ZOMBIE TEA PARTY

ARMAND ROSAMILIA

ZOMBIE TEA PARTY

Armand Rosamilia

Copyright 2011 by Armand Rosamilia

"First Settlement" originally appeared in *Twisted Dreams Magazine*

"Southern Barbeque", "Swim Out Past The Breakers" and "This Is The End" originally appeared in *Daily Bites of Flesh 2011*

"Blind In Texas" originally appeared in *State of Horror: Texas*

ISBN-13: 978-1466476370

ISBN-10: 1466476370

Published by Rymfire Undead

Cover art by Darlene Wanglund
http://blackfirex5656.deviantart.com/

Discover other Rymfire eBook titles by Armand Rosamilia
http://rymfireebooks.com/store.html

This eBook is licensed for your personal enjoyment only. This eBook may not be resold or given away to other people. If you would like to share this eBook with another person, please purchase an additional copy for each recipient. If you're reading this eBook and did not purchase it, or it was not purchased for your use only, then please return and purchase your own copy. Thank you for respecting the hard work of this author.

First Printing November 2011

Table of Contents

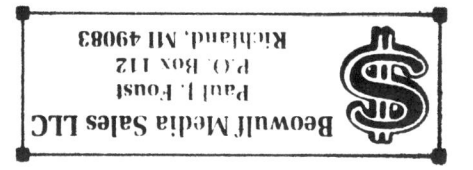

Zelebrity Money - Page 5
Zombies, Dogs and Old Bones - Page 13
First Settlement - Page 19
Manhattan Is A @#$%^& Island* - Page 21
Southern Barbeque - Page 33
Trail of The Undead - Page 35
Swim Out Past The Breakers - Page 39
Blind In Texas - Page 41
Caution, Smoke Ahead - Page 51
This Is The End - Page 63
Sanctuary - Page 65
Why I Write About Zombies - Page 75
"Dying Days" extreme zombie novella Preview - Page 77

Beowulf Media Sales LLC
Paul L. Foust
P.O. Box 112
Richland, MI 49083

Zelebrity Money

Ron Brown rubbed his hands and exhaled, staring at the contract and the multitude of zeros at the end. "Is this real?"

Bruster grinned and licked the cigar before depositing it back into his mouth. "Sure as shit it is, my boy." I just need the specimen in this office by eight sharp tomorrow morning, and then you can cash that fat check."

"I'll be here. I just need to talk to my aunt," Ron said and tried to smile but failed.

"I don't give a rat's ass how much you give to her, but the auction is in less than a week and I need to send out the catalog by tomorrow afternoon. If you're late or you pull out I can't list the specimen. Got it?"

"Got it."

Bruster fingered the check next to the contract. "All of this will be yours." He folded the check and put it in his shirt pocket. "Don't fuck this up, kid. I need this auction piece."

* * * * *

"No, and that's final."

"But, Aunt Maggie, this auctioneer promised us a hundred thousand dollars for him! You know how many zeros that is?"

Aunt Maggie shook her head and continued to watch her television.

Ron tried to figure it out but got bored with it. "A bunch, a bunch, I tell you. We could move back to the city and live like normal people."

"We are normal people, you don't think I'm normal?" she said and looked at him over her reading glasses. "Is there something wrong with me, Ronnie?"

"No, ma'am. It's just that I thought we could better ourselves."

"I'm as better as I need to be." Aunt Maggie waved her hands dramatically. "I have my own trailer, my own running water, an outhouse, miles and miles of protective fencing, and this television gets three channels. What else do I need? That money ain't worth the paper it's being printed on these days. People survive on goods and bartering."

"I could maybe ask for goods instead of money."

Aunt Maggie laughed. "What would you even ask for? Can you trade him in for a cow, and some chickens?"

Ron shrugged. "I could go back and ask."

She shook her head. "It's too dangerous nowadays. You need to stay home like I keep saying, and relax and watch the television and take a nap. A growing boy like you needs a nap every now and again. Your daddy took lots of naps when he was your age, and it did him good." Aunt Maggie shifted in her recliner. "Until he got bit, of course. But before that he would curl up right there on the couch and snore like a kitten."

"Daddy is gone. They're all gone, mostly. All we got is each other and him." Ron pointed at the backdoor. "What good is he?"

"He means everything to me," she said defensively.

"You never even knew him."

"How dare you." Aunt Maggie stood on old wobbly legs and headed to the kitchen. "I know more about him than his momma."

"It still ain't right." Ron decided to try for a new angle. "Some might call it kidnapping."

"No one would call it that, and you know it." Aunt Maggie got out her teapot and added water from the faucet. "Nothing you say will convince me any different. He's mine now, God's will and all that."

'What happens when he just, you know, fades away to nothing?"

"He won't, because I feed him. He's doing better, don't you think? His skin looks glossy."

"It looks gray."

"He's healthier than he's been in years, I'll tell you what. He just needs more meat," she said and put the teapot on the stove. "Be a dear and get your auntie the box of cookies from the pantry, the ones with the sprinkles on them."

Ron reluctantly got out the cookies, shoving two into his own mouth. It was hard enough getting cookies these days, and store-bought was getting scarcer than a two-headed chicken.

"Later you can hook up the video player and we'll watch one of his movies."

"I don't want to," Ronnie said as he put the box of cookies on the kitchen table. "I never cared for him."

Aunt Maggie clucked her tongue. "Don't you blaspheme in my house."

Ron was certain what he said had nothing to do with God or blaspheming, and this house was a beaten trailer in an empty trailer park, but he decided not to argue with her. Once she got something in her head you couldn't sway her, right or wrong.

Instead, he excused himself and went out the backdoor. The yard was gutted with chain-link fences, wooden fences, barbed wire, rusted cars pinned bumper to bumper, and chunks of the rest of the trailers nailed, glued and fitted together.

Amidst the chaos, in a ten by ten enclosed area He stood.

His dark mop of hair was falling out in clumps, his moustache covered in dried blood. His eyes were bloodshot, his mouth a red slick of gore.

Ron turned away and stared into the distance at nothing, since there wasn't a darn thing to see. The neighbors had either been eaten during the initial plague or simply packed up their meager possessions and fled. He didn't know where they'd gone, but none had returned.

Aunt Maggie truly ruled the trailer park. The nearest city was Jupiter, where Aunt Maggie had visited often. Where she got Him.

"Come back in and set up the thingy for me so I can watch *Navajo Joe*. It was his first Spaghetti Western, you know." She stood in the doorway, the teapot screaming in the kitchen behind her.

"Yes, I know. You told me all about it."

"Still a classic after all these years."

"It's an old, old movie and I hate cowboys and Indians movies. Can't we watch a comedy?"

"Later we will. I like to start my week with some of his westerns and older material and watch his career progress. After dinner we'll put on *100 Rifles* and *Sam Whiskey*. Come on in before something sees you."

"It would take them an hour to get through your maze."

She smiled at that, very proud of the work she'd put into her makeshift fortress. It was true; nothing could get through some of the obstacles.

"The gator is still out there, you know. He might get ya," she said and laughed. "Get it, gator?"

"Yes," Ron said and trudged back up into the kitchen.

"Maybe later we can skip ahead and watch him as Bobby 'Gator' McCluskey. Sound like an evening?"

"Not really." Ron took the wailing teapot off the stove. "You're worried about me drawing attention but you let the steam whistle blow for an hour."

"Pour me a strong cup. There's my bottle in the cabinet."

Ron found the Irish Whisky and added a generous helping to her cup, hoping it would get her to pass out in her chair so they didn't have to watch the movies.

No such luck.

Aunt Maggie made them a dinner of roasted potatoes and canned corn, but she took the remaining meat from the ice chest and tossed it over the fence for Him to eat.

"What a waste," Ron cried. "He doesn't even appreciate it. He eats like an animal."

"He'll get better."

"No, he won't. Eventually he'll break loose and eat one of us like the rest of them do."

"He's not like them others. You can see the intelligence in his eyes. He doesn't growl as much as the other ones did, and he doesn't spend his days trying to escape. He seems… gentle, don't you think?"

Ron put his hand near the fence and wasn't surprised when He charged and tried to sink his deadly teeth into his palm. "Don't seem so gentle to me."

"I don't blame him. You're being cruel, tempting him like that. Leave him be, and let's go watch some movies."

Ron stared into the bloody eyes and shuddered. He'd kill and eat them both if given a chance.

* * * * *

The moaning woke Ron up. His neck was stiff from falling asleep on the couch during the opening credits to *Skullduggery*, a movie that he hated.

Aunt Maggie was snoring softly in her chair, the VCR tapes in a neat stack on her TV tray. She was wrapped in her favorite blanket, three pillows propped around her.

He smelled bad. His immediate response was to lunge at Ron, who simply pushed with the bear-catcher. Before he knew it Ron had moved him out of the kitchen and into the living room.

Aunt Maggie screamed when she was bitten.

Ron let Him finish his feast, while His movie played in the background, before grabbing him with the device and moving toward the front door and a rich payday.

Zombies, Dogs and Old Bones

John William Murphy heard Gidget barking on the front porch and cringed, eliciting another round of popping in his weak knees. "I'm getting' too old fer this shit," he drawled.

As if in response the dog, a tiny little mixed breed John and Sue had rescued years ago, began to bark again at a fevered pitch, scratching at the door jam.

"Cut it out, you mangy mutt!" John yelled. "Getting' too old. I'm fallin' apart at the damn seams." He fell heavily into his favorite chair.

Through the boarded-up windows a slant of failing sunlight poked through, spotting his well-worn carpet. His aged hand went to the remote control on the TV tray next to him. He could almost hear the bones creaking and clacking under his taut skin.

The first four channels he surfed on TV were all news interruptions: ZOMBIE ATTACK, UNDEAD RAVAGING NEW YORK, and IS THIS THE END OF THE WORLD?

"Damn straight it's the end of the world." John tried to get comfortable in his worn leather chair. He couldn't find a spot where his bones didn't feel like cracking off and falling to the dusty carpet. "Ain't there a damn college football game on anymore?" John was getting sick of these sensational reports about creatures roaming the cities and countryside, eating people and destroying civilization. All he wanted was to see his beloved Gators playing some ball.

Gidget banged against the door on the porch, shaking the lock. John thought he heard wood splintering on that one, and knew before long he'd have to do something about it. For now he was content to change the channel and ignore the negatives. He came upon an episode of *Cops* he was sure he'd seen already and sunk down into the chair.

John William Murphy dreamed of his young bride, Sue, running through a field toward him like in an old movie they showed on Turner Classic Movies Channel, her dark hair whipping in the wind and her arms outstretched. She was beaming, her smile as wide as her eyes. *Fear.* He realized the look on her face was one of terror, her mouth caught in a scream and her eyes bulging with fear. Her skin was mottled in places and her hair began to flake from her gray scalp. He was paralyzed as she came within ten yards of him, trampling over the daisies and turning them aflame in her wake. Her fingernails charred and dripped from her dead hands and she fell to her broken knees only inches from him. John could hear her bones snapping with the strain of her weight and she bent unnaturally at her hips, falling back. Her ruined face pointed skyward and her lips moved, a guttural sound escaping through cracked teeth. "The dog is driving me crazy," she breathed her last.

John woke with a start. The room was dark except for another flashing newscast about zombies burning down the White House and destroying the L.A. Forum.

Gidget was still barking and probably hadn't stopped since John took his nap. He didn't feel refreshed; in fact, he felt more tired than when he began the day.

By his watch it was nearing five o'clock. Time to make some dinner, even though he didn't feel hungry at all.

There was a can of chicken noodle soup in the cabinet and a loaf of stale bread. "Not much fer choices, eh?"

While the soup cooked on the stove John gingerly sat down at the kitchen table and folded his throbbing hands. He only glanced at the dog bite on his wrist, now purple and swollen. It had stopped hurting last night, eve though it was angry and probably infected. At some point the bandage wrapping he'd applied had come off.

Outside he heard a distant siren from a police cruiser and stood to investigate. "No damn use," he blurted. Last night he'd boarded up the windows and back door. He didn't know if he really believed in these zombie attacks and if it could even come close to his little town, but why take the chance.

He remembered the police officer who had come to his door yesterday morning. The young man had reminded him of his son, John Junior. He was clean-cut and official-sounding, but he had that air of mischief and that likeable twinkle in his eye. Junior had done his fair share of craziness in his younger years, but nothing bad enough to keep him off of the police force himself. "Sir, there's been an – " the officer had glanced down before resuming, "-there's been an accident not far from here, and we're asking all residents to, as a precaution, you see, stay inside the house and keep your pets and family members inside until the problem is resolved."

"What kind of problem?" John had asked at the time. He never watched TV except for the History Channel or reality shows about cops and accidents.

The officer had looked away. "People are coming back."

"What people?"

"Dead people."

"Yer shittin' me, boy. Is Junior trying to pull a fast one on his old man?"

The officer had looked at John, his official demeanor replaced by tears. "I wish I was, sir. I wish I was." The officer wiped his eyes and got hold of himself. "I would suggest you boarding up the windows, turning the news on, and pray to God that this isn't really happening."

Once John saw the first newscast, he went to the garage and pulled out every last board, two by four and nail he could muster. His hands were hurting by the time he'd finished. He was getting too old fer this shit.

Gidget had watched him for the most part, following him from window to window outside and sitting in the shade while John worked. When it was time to go inside and secure the screen porch and front door, Gidget was missing.

"Gidget, Gidget! Where are ya, damn dog! Get inside."

John was about to shut the door and nail it shut to the frame when Gidget appeared, little tail wagging and his tiny ears pointing to the sky. "Where ya been? Get yer butt inside." John reached down to grab the dog but he must've spooked him, because Gidget sunk his sharp teeth into John's wrist.

"You little bastard!" John kicked at the dog, which jumped just out of reach. The skin had been broken, blood dripping down John's arm. "You little bastard," he repeated.

The dog had spent the night on the front porch, barking and whining. "It's too late fer ya now, Gidget. I'm not pulling them damn boards off of the door. I'm too tired."

John turned the soup off, pulled out his favorite bowl, and went searching for some crackers. Sue always broke three crackers in his soup before she served it. "God, I miss that woman." He didn't find the crackers but a half-empty bottle of Crown Royal hidden in the top cabinet made him smile.

As he entered the living room he was disgusted to see more images of zombies on the screen. "Enough already."

He put the soup and Crown Royal bottle on his TV tray and dropped into his chair. He grabbed the remote control but smiled before he could flip to the next channel, turning up the volume over the barking of the dog.

A news reporter, impeccably dressed and solemn, held a microphone and moved his free hand dramatically like he was a host on a game show. "You see behind me a live shot of the living dead, shuffling up Broadway. No, this isn't some theatrical dramatization to garner ticket sales for a new play."

The camera closed in on the three lead zombies, bloody and disheveled. They slid across the pavement on broken ankles. Their glazed-over eyes were locked on the reporter.

What had made John smile was the scroll at the bottom of the screen that kept flashing: BREAKING NEWS… ZOMBIE FROM MICHAEL JACKSON VIDEO IS NOW A ZOMBIE.

"Show us the Michael Jackson zombie, damnit!" John said to the TV. He wondered if it was the lead female in the "Thriller" video, or if it was just some boring random video from after that. "I wonder if the damn thing can still do that zombie dance."

John put his finger in the scalding soup but felt nothing. He always tested his soup with a finger, which drove Sue crazy. He dipped his spoon into the bowl coming up with a mouthful. As soon as it hit his tongue he spit it out. It tasted weird; different… it didn't taste edible. It was a bitter taste in his mouth, but when he took a swig of the alcohol it had the same taste and he spit it out and put the bottle back down. "Damn shame."

The screen now went to a taped segment with a scene from the "Thriller" video and an opaque oval over one of the dancers in the background. Apparently he had become an actual zombie and the local news was ecstatic to be doing an exclusive breaking news segment about it.

A loud banging against the front door startled John. "Damn dog." A part of him felt bad for leaving Gidget outside all night, especially with all of the trouble in the world, but he'd be damned if he was going to get bit again. If Sue were here she'd know the right thing to do. He imagined her scolding Gidget and whacking her behind with a rolled newspaper.

Another thud made the door shake. The dog didn't let up the barking.

"I've had enough," John mumbled. He was getting tired now, so weak. He wanted to take another nap.

First things first.

He went back into the kitchen, although it was getting harder to take each step now. After what seemed like an hour he struggled to the pantry and found his lock box. Setting it on the kitchen table he opened the top just as a wave of nausea overtook him. Despite not eating in who knew how long, John vomited on the floor beside him and fell to one knee. He wiped puke and blood from his mouth as his head spun. He could hear his heart struggling in his chest, pounding to the rhythm of Gidget barking. Without looking he reached up and pulled the loaded handgun from the box.

He threw up twice more on his way to the front door, picking up the hammer as he went along. He fell heavily against the door and tried to keep from passing out, but his eyes unfocused.

Gidget slamming against the door and another loud commotion woke him from his resting spot in front of the door. He rose and used the hammer effortlessly to yank the boards from the door. He kept the gun in his hand.

It was daytime, and the sun blinded him for a second. Gidget was on the front steps, in a sitting position and suddenly quiet. She stared up at John without blinking.

"Mister Murphy, get back inside," the young police officer was yelling from the street. He stood behind his police cruiser, legs spread and holding his police-issue weapon before him.

A zombie was moving toward the officer, dark hair coated in gore. Her clothes were tatters, caked with mud and harboring maggots.

"Lock your door and bar the window," the officer said again.

John noticed that the street on his block was deserted, and several of his neighbor's houses had been torched.

The zombie glanced at John and stopped shuffling forward.

John raised his handgun and remembered his Army training, pulling the trigger and getting a direct shot between the eyes.

As the officer hit the ground, blood pouring from the wound, Sue walked slowly up the front walkway.

"It's been too long, baby," John said. He wanted to smile but rigor mortis was setting into his jaw line.

Sue came back home and Gidget, her fur coated in blood and her teeth beginning to fall out, came in behind her masters.

First Settlement

I hope this letter finds Sir John White, my father-in-law and governor of Roanoke Island, before it is too late.
3rd Day of July, 1589

The Indian was dying. I stared at the gaping wounds: one across his dark chest, another on his left shoulder, a rip where his right ear should have been. His eyes were bloodshot and I choked back my last meal. "He's been mauled," I said quietly to Horace Benjamin, the lone physician on Roanoke Island.

"Aye. But the bites are smaller than a cat native to this region." Horace put a wet strip of cloth on the Indian's forehead. "I'd say he was bitten by another man."

I scoffed. "That makes no sense. What man would do that?"

"What man would let him?" Horace asked.

"Virginia, get back here," my wife, Eleanor, yelled to our two-year old pride and joy. Virginia was the first baby born in this new world. She watched just as the Indian stopped breathing on the oak table.

"Dear, can you excuse us? We –"

Virginia screamed as the Indian slid off the table and dropped upon her tiny frame. Before I could react the Indian had drawn blood from my daughter. Horace charged and the Indian gouged his neck with his teeth, a spray of blood following.

I am ashamed to say that I panicked and ran from the building, clutching my wife's hand in mine. I yelled for weapons and called my fellow colonists to my side.

By then it was too late. The Indian, Horace, and Virginia burst from the house and fell upon former allies. Even as rifles were fired I knew it was hopeless.

"What is the matter with them?" Eleanor cried.

"They are dead," I whispered, fear rooting me to the spot. I watched as those killed rose and joined in the massacre.

Hand in hand, Eleanor and I ran to our home near the north gate of the fort. Leaving without supplies in the midst of this infernal summer would be suicide; a few items and we would be off.

We packed hastily and slipped through the abandoned gate, the screams and firing weapons filling the air. Before entering the woods I carved CROATOAN onto a palisade as a sign to you, knowing that I had failed your daughter. Eleanor and I would seek help with the Indian tribe.

We moved into the woods slowly.

"Listen." The gunfire had ceased. There were over one hundred colonists. I prayed to God that more had escaped.

I stopped at a large tree and began to carve. "After this we'll be off."

When Eleanor didn't answer me I turned toward her. Virginia, our precious daughter, had clamped her filthy blood-caked teeth onto her mother's thigh.

I ran like a coward. I hope that a search party will be able to decipher CRO on the tree as to my destination.

I also pray that the dead Indian was not a Croatoan.

Annanais Dare

Manhattan Is A @#$%^& Island*

"Who are you with?" the skinhead asked Buddy, the shotgun pointing at his chest. This was no normal lunatic Buddy had dealt with over the last seven months – ever since the world turned upside down and the dead annihilated large portions of mankind – but a far more menacing opponent: one with a steady grip on a loaded weapon.

The skinhead repeated the question. Buddy could see the telltale Swastika tattoos and racist slogans inked to his body, especially with no shirt on and only red suspenders covering his upper torso. His head looked freshly shaven.

Buddy could've kicked himself in the ass for being so vain after all these weeks, and shaving his head again. *With survival at the top of the list, you'd think I'd worry about food and drink. But there I was a few days ago, scrounging through an abandoned drugstore for shaving cream and razors,* he thought bitterly. With most residents of Manhattan either dead or already escaped, it was fairly easy to move from place to place. The bridges had been destroyed by either the zombies or the military trying to contain the outbreak, and for the most part it was quiet.

The shotgun's cold touch brought Buddy back to the present. "I asked you a question. Do you want to die?"

Buddy didn't think he wanted to die, so he tried his best to smile. If it wasn't for the fact that this bastard had a gun pointing at his chest, he would have laughed. Buddy was squatting down in a fast food restaurant and eating packets of ketchup, with warm soda staining his new T-shirt and his new Timberland boots – Tims as the kids called them – and his backpack of survival gear was close at hand. The bag contained three handguns, but Buddy must have glanced in that direction because the skinhead pushed at him with the shotgun barrel and kicked the backpack away.

"I'm by myself," Buddy blurted before the skinhead coated the dirty floor with a mix of blood, heart and ketchup.

"Who are you with?" he repeated.

"Look around. I'm here by myself, trying to eat," Buddy said weakly.

He stared for a long moment and Buddy thought he was going to shoot him. He didn't know too much about shotguns and prayed to God that he wouldn't be able to blow a huge hole in his chest with it pressed against his new T-shirt.

"There's a war going on in my streets," the skinhead said matter-of-factly.

Buddy wanted to laugh but decided against it. *No shit there's a war going on, you fucking idiot! The damn zombies are killing us!* "I know there is," he managed to get out.

"Then who are you with?"

"You," Buddy answered, *or any person holding a gun to my chest, for Christ sake.*

The skinhead pulled the shotgun away from Buddy and glanced at the broken doors to the place. "We control this sector, from Houston to 14th Street. I'm waiting for my brothers to get here so we can clear this sector of Inferiors and the enemy."

Inferiors? "Well, I'm neither of those things. I'm just minding my own business and trying to eat some ketchup."

"There's a deli about two blocks from here with meat that hasn't rotted completely through yet. I made a sub yesterday," he said. "What's your name?"

"Friends call me Buddy," Buddy said and rose slowly. He didn't want him getting jittery or doing anything stupid like cover the walls with brains. "I've been moving from building to building the last few weeks, trying to find a decent amount of food and keeping as far away from the water as I can." In the past month or so the zombies had begun to walk across the river in search of prey.

"This area is picked clean. We rounded up all of the canned goods and drink we could find and stored them at a place called Bleeker Bill's," he said. "I'm Kevin, and I'll be your lieutenant from now on. We need to move if we're going to outrun the enemy."

I'm eating from ketchup packets with a stockpile of food around the damn corner. Canned food did sound good, but being enlisted with this guy was not reason enough for Buddy. "If it's all the same, I was going to head east and try for the Manhattan Bridge."

Kevin shook his head. "The bridges have been destroyed. Manhattan Bridge is gone, the fucking Brooklyn Bridge is a pile of rubble, the Williamsburg, Queensboro, G.W.B. is gone… the fuckers destroyed them all and trapped us here."

"Then the tunnels –"

"The tunnels are filled in, destroyed. The bastards punched holes and flooded them. The Lincoln Tunnel, the Queens-

Midtown, the Holland, the Brooklyn-Battery, is all underwater now. Have you seen the Statue of Liberty?"

Bile rose in Buddy's throat. *This was worse than I thought.* "No," he said.

"Neither has anyone else." He pointed the shotgun at Buddy one-handed and grimaced. "They somehow took down the Statue of Liberty. I'm not going to cry over it, that damn place was a beacon for all of the Inferiors to come to our country and take up our jobs anyway. But still… she was a big bitch, and now she's sleeping in the bay."

"I was hoping to get back to my family in Brooklyn."

"No sleep 'til Brooklyn," Kevin said with a laugh. "Brooklyn is fucked same as Manhattan. The enemy came up through the sewers and from the rivers and streams and bay. They dragged people down into the water and ate them." He paused. "Or did worse to them."

Buddy laughed uneasily. While he had been a survivor for this long, it was because of his penchant to run as far away from trouble as fast as possible. He had never actually seen the enemy up close. He simply heard the newscasts while there were some – before the power went out far and near – and noticed less and less people around. The ones that survived the longest told horror stories like this guy, but it seemed like they were getting crazier and crazier. "I actually haven't seen the enemy," Buddy said simply.

Suddenly Kevin charged across the restaurant and put his forearm in Buddy's face. "I have," he spat and tapped his forearm with his other hand, right below a tattoo of Jesus. There, in concentric circles, were three bruised bite marks. "Fucker latched onto my arm and started chomping. It sprang right from the Hudson River with a hundred others. They tore into my brothers and I fought them off."

"When was the last time you saw your brothers?" Buddy asked.

Kevin shook his head and grabbed Buddy roughly by the back of his neck, putting his forehead against Buddy's and staring into his eyes. "*Our* brothers, Buddy, *our* brothers. We need to find them. We need to keep control of Greenwich Village, clear out the Inferiors and fight the enemy until the death."

Buddy gently pulled his head away from Kevin's but he was still standing nearly on top of him, their chests scant inches away from each other. Kevin smelled of sweat and smoke. "The last time you saw your… our brothers was at the attack near the Hudson River?"

Kevin nodded. "Yes, but I know that there were survivors."

"How?"

"I've seen many Inferior bodies in the streets and in empty buildings. I came across a fire at NYU four days ago and there were dozens of Inferiors piled there burning. The enemy doesn't do that, they don't burn us. They eat us."

Buddy still wasn't a hundred percent sure who the Inferiors were, but he assumed it was everyone this Aryan was against: blacks, Hispanics, Asians… shit; this guy was against most New York residents. The Big Apple wasn't called the Great Melting Pot for nothing. Buddy decided to keep all of that to himself for now. "Is there any escape from Manhattan then?"

"Why would you want to leave? There are plenty of streets that are untouched by the zombies, and we have a large store of foodstuffs to last us months until the threat is eradicated. Besides, I haven't seen a living Inferior in days and I'm sure our brothers are out searching for us."

Buddy couldn't resist. "Aren't there more colorful words to use besides Inferiors?"

Kevin motioned for Buddy to follow him out the door, and with the shotgun casually pointed at him Buddy decided to comply. "We don't use the 'N' word anymore, since they call each other that. I can't get over that, by the way. Why use a word that we call you to point out your inferiority? And call each other and put it in your shitty rap music."

Buddy had no answer for him and decided not to say anything stupid. He wasn't prejudiced, and he was raised better than to think that he was better than anyone. He just wanted to keep his nose clean and try to survive in this fucked up madhouse.

They moved out into the street and stood in the deserted road, watching and waiting for something. At least, that's what Kevin did, one hand covering the sun's glare while his other hand propped the shotgun onto his shoulder. Out in the direct light Buddy could see that Kevin wasn't much older than twenty, but he looked haggard. He guessed he hadn't slept much either in the last few weeks. At least he had eaten.

"Any chance we can shoot down to Bleeker Street and get some food?" Buddy asked.

Kevin turned suddenly and smashed him across the jaw with the shotgun. He was stunned to say the least. When Buddy came to his senses he was down on one knee and leaning across the grill of an SUV. "We eat when I say we eat," Kevin spat. He put his hand up. "Did you hear that?"

Buddy rubbed his jaw and wished he had a weapon to shoot this bald-fuck's head off. "Hear what?"

Kevin shushed him and turned in a circle, staring above at the tops of the buildings.

Buddy didn't hear anything but he didn't say another word. He didn't feel like getting cracked in the face again by this madman. And he was still hungry.

There was a slight tremor underneath them in the street, followed by a grating sound fifty yards down the avenue. "Shit," Buddy whispered, as a sewer grate shot five feet into the air and crashed down where the noise had occurred.

Kevin yelled for Buddy to follow him but he was right on his ass as they moved in the opposite direction. They skirted 7th Avenue and turned onto Bleeker, the street underneath them groaning and buckling. Buddy nearly tripped twice over debris but managed to stay close to Kevin and his shotgun, hoping that whatever was underneath them could be outrun. *I just need to outrun Kevin,* Buddy thought humorously, remembering an old joke about two hunters having to outrun a bear. *I need to outrun this bastard and hope his death saves my life.* Buddy wondered if he would be able to do it if it came down to it. *Could I let another human being die in order to save my skin?*

Who the hell are you trying to kid? Shit yes you'll do it to save your sorry ass.

"In here, we can make our stand until our brother's return," Kevin said and kicked in a door at random. They took the tight, dusty steps two at a time until they reached the third floor landing, where Kevin kicked in another door and they entered a dark apartment.

By habit Buddy tried the light switch, even though the electricity had gone out months ago. The room reeked of rotten food and decaying plants. Buddy was disappointed to find that all of the furniture and knickknacks were still in place, if a bit dusty. *I guess I was looking for a scene out of a movie, with broken furniture and a chalked-out body in the living room with spent shells at my feet,* he thought.

"This apartment is nicer than mine in Brooklyn, I'll tell you that," Buddy said and sat down on the couch. "Now what?"

"We wait until the street calms down. Those creatures are following us. As long as we remain quiet we should be fine." Kevin sat on the chair opposite Buddy and placed the shotgun across his lap.

"Mind if I turn on the television?" Buddy asked. He was trying to be a smartass but was also scared of the way Kevin was staring at him, his mouth slightly ajar and his eyes locked on his.

From the third floor they couldn't hear anything going on downstairs, which was just as well. *For all we knew, the Four Horsemen of The Apocalypse could have been saddling up in front of CBGB's and preparing to come fetch us, driving the last of the punks and street people before them,* Buddy decided.

Buddy's thoughts of the Ramones, Talking Heads and prostitutes were interrupted by a banging in the kitchen.

Kevin did one of those silent point-at-him-point-at-you hand signals that caused Buddy to sit up, but he put the stop sign on with his hand and Buddy stayed like a good doggy.

Kevin crept quietly toward the closed kitchen door, shotgun leading. Buddy stood and moved as far across the living room as he could go. He'd seen enough movies to know that when Kevin opened that door Satan himself was liable to take wing and crush them like grapes.

Buddy scanned the room for a weapon and came up empty unless he wanted to use a broken chair leg, but he didn't think it would be nice to break the furniture since the owners had taken such care of everything.

It occurred to him that the owners were now zombie food just as Kevin pushed the door open with the shotgun.

There were no flap of demon wings, no dragon breath burning them to death, nothing more than a metallic tink coming from the pantry. Kevin turned sideways and glanced at Buddy, motioning him forward.

"I don't have a weapon," Buddy whispered. There was no way he was going into Hell's kitchen without something to defend himself with.

Kevin reached into his left Doc Marten and pulled out a small handgun. He tossed it to Buddy, who groaned when he almost dropped it. Without another pause Kevin moved into the kitchen and the door closed behind him.

Several thoughts formed in Buddy's head. *I could easily walk out the front door and charge down the stairs and get away from this lunatic. I could expend every bullet in the gun into the closed kitchen door and hope that I hit the racist fucker. I could get into a position and fire on him when he came back out.*

Instead, he stood with his arm and gun extended, trembling fingers as he pointed at the door and his legs buckled slightly. He'd never held a gun before this madness started, and the three guns that he owned – *used to own before I left my backpack*, he thought – had never been fired by him. Buddy wondered if the gun he'd been given was even loaded, but didn't want to stop and check.

Thunk.

Something heavy fell in the kitchen, followed by silence. The hush that followed was more disconcerting than the noise and Buddy teetered again on shaking knees. He needed to get to that food storage as soon as possible, but his brain refused to help move his body.

Buddy tried to call out to Kevin but his throat was like sandpaper and no sound would escape. He managed to shuffle both feet forward but that was all. A wild thought occurred to him to charge into the kitchen, gun blazing and killing everything that moved.

Instead, he took five long steps to the front door, and pointed the gun at the kitchen. The door was ajar from Kevin's kick but closed and he worried that it was lodged into the jam and he was trapped. Buddy stood for a long moment and couldn't decide what to do.

When he heard the first shotgun blast he made up his mind. By the time he was back on Bleeker he had counted at least three other gunshots, most likely from another handgun Kevin had in his other boot.

Again Buddy was expecting a swarm of zombies to be filling the street, but instead there was nothing new on the deserted avenue. He took several steps toward Bleeker Bill's and hesitated. *Was there a swarm of skinheads like Kevin waiting for me there?*

His stomach growled and he wanted to scream. He knew he couldn't go much longer eating ketchup packets, but he needed to stay focused and get a game plan. He needed his backpack and the three handguns. If nothing else he knew it would give him peace of mind when he tried to get to the food. *I should have asked Kevin how many 'brothers' he thought were left behind there, if any.*

Buddy couldn't remember if Kevin had mentioned anyone there or if he was talking about before the slaughter on the docks. He didn't want to go all the way down Bleeker to find out. *I think I only have a few more hours before I'll be too weak to run from the undead or the skinheads.*

Buddy stood in the street for perhaps an hour, trying to think straight. He couldn't. Then he sat for a time, right there in the middle of the avenue where hundreds of people had moved about months ago. Band flyers, stapled haphazardly to any available space, swayed in the breeze. He decided to go back for his stuff.

The fast food restaurant was just as he left it: booths overturned, the counter cracked and strewn with debris, and a neat pile of ketchup packets – some opened, others still waiting for him – in the center of the dining area.

His backpack was missing.

Buddy walked around the floor and realized that he still held the gun. He was glad, because if another skinhead appeared and had his backpack he was getting a warning shot to the face. *Did Kevin take it when we met?* Buddy didn't think so, but he was so damn hungry at this point that maybe he had slung it over his shoulder. *Shit!*

The backpack held every meager thing that Buddy owned, but right now he could only remember the handguns. *I guess this one will have to do;* he thought as he dropped the clip from the gun and cursed. It was empty.

A frantic search of the front and back rooms brought him nothing new except a box of moldy hamburger buns and more condiment packets. Without fanfare he sat behind the counter, cried softly, and ate mustard and ketchup until he gagged.

Darkness took Manhattan and Buddy watched the sun fall from his vantage point, cursing another night in this city. As a child his grandfather was fond of telling him that New York was the City That Never Sleeps. Despite the lack of citizens he still agreed. He still felt the rhythmic pulse of the silent streets, the undercurrent as if something big was about to happen… and he prayed to a God he hadn't prayed to since junior high that the something big wasn't going to involve him.

He must have slept through the night. A thin, sickly-yellow shaft of sunlight woke him from his dreamless slumber and he rose slowly and stretched his aching muscles. His neck was sore from sleeping in a sitting position against the wall and he heard his back crack as he raised his hands over his head.

That's when Buddy saw the… thing… watching him. It was bloody and rotting, with large oval eyes that gleamed like marbles. Covered in dirty and shredded clothes, large chunks of flesh dangling from its torso, it was on the other side of the counter. *It isn't moving*, Buddy thought and took a step to the right and the door.

The zombie scrambled to intercept him, those eyes locked onto his. Its mouth opened and a stream of dark gore dribbled from between rows of sharp teeth.

Buddy held up the handgun like a small club. He couldn't shoot the creature but he could bludgeon it to death.

Something fell behind him, sounding like a shotgun blast. Buddy lunged forward and the zombie came at him. Buddy swung the gun and connected with its head, knocking it down. Without waiting to find out what was behind him he ran for the door. Three more of the zombies appeared inside the building but he didn't stop to see what they looked like. He was a hundred feet down the road before he stopped to catch his breath. There might have been a dozen of them in there with him. *That's how people die, overwhelmed by them.*

The street shook and Buddy moved away as a chunk of pavement rose up a foot and then collapsed again. Beneath him it rose again and he realized that there was something underneath him – something big – following him down the street. He remembered seeing Kevin Bacon in that *Tremors* movie as a kid and being scared of the giant worms under the ground that sensed movement. He stopped, but the ground underneath him shook violently. *I'm no Kevin Bacon,* he thought. He ran into the nearest open doorway and tried to find a way out the back.

Buddy wondered how his heart had been pounding so long and so loud. He felt the shrapnel from the shotgun blast, hot against his arms and legs, as it ricocheted against the wall to his left without hearing it. Before he knew it he was down, covered in dust and wreckage from the blast.

"Stay down," Kevin said through the haze. Buddy glanced up and could see his silhouette coming toward him. He wanted to run but his body wouldn't cooperate. His stomach growled again and he realized that if he had a weapon on him right now he'd most likely gut himself, a big fuck you to his hunger.

Kevin stood over him with his reloaded shotgun. "Did I hit you?"

Buddy wanted to say, 'of course, you stupid racist motherfucker!' but instead he groaned. If he had the strength he would have wrestled him for the shotgun and put the damn thing in his mouth or begged him to kill him already.

"I think I got two of them," Kevin said and stepped over and past Buddy. "We need to get back to Bleeker Bill's and get you some food."

Before Buddy's numbing mind could respond Kevin was lifting Buddy by his charred arms. His appendages were scorched and blistering but not burnt beyond repair. All he needed was a doctor or a first aid kit. Buddy wondered idly if his backpack contained one. Not that he'd ever find it again.

As if reading his thought, Kevin handed it to Buddy. "I took one of the handguns and used a band-aid." He pointed at his temple, bloody and dirt-caked. "Everything else is there, you can check."

"What?" Buddy managed to squeak and shielded his eyes from the weak sunlight as they went back outside.

"After the attack in that apartment I circled back to the restaurant, figuring we'd rendezvous there. When you didn't return right away I grabbed your gear and found a rooftop to sleep on. I heard the commotion in the restaurant and came back for you. You would have done the same for me, brother."

Not a chance. "Of course. Can we get something to eat?"

Kevin slapped him on the back hard and he winced in pain. "Let's go get some grub. The rest of the brothers will be happy to meet you."

As they walked down the now-silent street Buddy casually reached into his backpack and pulled a handgun out. He was praying that Kevin had been straight with him and didn't unload them, but he couldn't pull it out here and check without him growing suspicious.

They made it to the front of Bleeker Bill's without incident.

"It's quiet," Kevin said and hesitated at the door.

"Too quiet," Buddy whispered and giggled. He had an image of Shrek and Donkey saying that and knew he needed food fast.

"Stop," Kevin finally said and Buddy stifled his laughs with an over-cooked hand. He was actually glad for the hunger pains and the oncoming delusional state since the pain of the burns wasn't too bad.

The door opened with a push of the shotgun and Kevin entered slowly. The front room was immaculate, with records, CDs, punk band T-shirts and posters neatly piled in displays and on the walls. Sunlight streamed into a good chunk of the store, casting everything in an early-morning glow. Buddy imagined a time not too long ago, with Gothic chicks and punk rock boys converging on this music landmark. He could hear Agnostic Front, Murphy's Law, and Biohazard blasting on the speakers, harkening back to the golden age of music in these parts. He felt older than his thirty-five years at that moment.

Buddy followed Kevin at a safe distance to a closed back door, holding the handgun in front of him but away from his back. He didn't know why. *If push came to shove I'd blast a hole the size of Yankee Stadium in his bald head,* Buddy thought.

Kevin glanced back at Buddy once and motioned for him to be quiet. For some reason Buddy took that as an excuse to giggle again. Kevin shook his head and entered the stockroom of the store.

It was empty save for boxes of new merchandise and a small table and three chairs. Kevin stared dumbly at the empty shelves to either side of them and waved the shotgun. "It was here, right here."

He tore into the closest box, spilling Marilyn Manson T-shirts onto the floor. "I don't understand. These shelves were packed with cans of food."

"I guess your brothers took them."

"And went where?" Kevin turned on Buddy and that flash of crazy was in his eyes again like when they'd first met. "There's nowhere to go. Manhattan is a fucking island! The enemies are all around us."

The front windows shattered at that moment, followed by the crash of the front door. Buddy didn't even bother to turn around.

Kevin pushed past him and fired the shotgun. "Come on, you dead bastards! I'll take on the entire Five Boroughs if I have to."

"You probably will," Buddy said. He sat down on the floor and covered his ears as Kevin followed shot after shot with maniacal curses.

"My new Tims are getting wet," Buddy said with a chuckle. The floor was covered in blood.

When the first of the undead pushed into the room, shaved head, Swastika tattoos and dead eyes, Buddy wasn't surprised.

Kevin loaded and reloaded his many guns, firing and blaring.

As seven more of the creatures appeared Buddy put the gun in his mouth and prayed that if there was a God that a bullet would be in the chamber. *I only need one.*

Kevin was silenced in mid-scream behind Buddy and dozens of the creatures, former brothers, appeared.

Buddy closed his eyes and pulled the trigger, giggling as the bullet tore through his brain.

Southern Barbeque

"Friends In Low Places" was so loud in his pickup truck that Jesse didn't notice the gunshots. When he stopped at Bunnell's Meats he didn't notice the burning train on the tracks just up the road intersecting Route 100. He was too busy humming his Garth Brooks tune as he grabbed a cart and entered the store.

Today he'd have the clan over for some delicious Southern barbeque: grilled pork steaks, blackened fish, barbequed green beans, corn on the cob, and mom's potato salad. Sue and Teddy would be bringing over some beer and that bit of moonshine they'd gotten from the folks in Georgia. Stella and the kids would add sweet potato pie to the table.

Jesse waltzed up to the meat section and selected a few items. There would be sixteen to twenty members of the family there today so he needed plenty.

Something was wrong. He took off his Stetson and rubbed his balding head. The store was empty of customers. That was never the case, even this early on a Sunday.

"Hello? Emma?" he finally called. Nothing.

He finished shopping and got to the checkout. No one was around. "Shit, gal, I'm in a hurry here. Got me a family event in a few hours and need to get this meat to the grill." Jesse checked the office and the stockroom but it was vacant.

"I'll leave this here on the counter," he yelled and felt foolish. Who was he talking to? He left some cash after figuring about what he owed, bagged it and wheeled the cart outside.

"I'll be damned." He noticed the train down the block and the pawn shop across the street with the windows busted out.

Jesse got back in his pickup after adding the bags to the front seat. He turned down Garth but didn't turn it off. After all, it was Garth.

Around the corner the church was aflame. Jesse slammed on the brakes and went up on the lawn. Without thinking he rushed from his pickup truck and ran to it. Reverend Minor was a good man and he hoped he wasn't trapped inside.

The doors to the church burst open and two teens exited slowly.

"Are you OK?" Jesse asked.

They ignored his question, lumbering toward him.

Something was wrong, very wrong. Both had long, tattered hair and wore disgusting T-shirts with demons and evil things on them. Slayer and Cannibal Corpse? Jesse had never heard of them, but assumed they were heavy metal or rap groups. Crap. "Did you do this? Devil worshipping maggots!"

They came at him, slow and steady. Jesse fended them off, aware that they stunk to High Heaven. They were bloody and rotten and… dead.

Jesse was stunned. These scarecrow hairbag freaks were glassy-eyed and not breathing, yet they gripped him with steely dead hands and dragged him, screaming, into the burning church while Garth swooned on in the pickup truck and the barbeque meat slowly rotted in the heat.

Trail of the Undead

Jim Frost pointed the Remington Model 700 ADL at the couple coming up the trail and smiled. "Stop or I'll pull this here trigger and kill you within a blink," he said in his best hillbilly drawl.

William Boone, known to his few remaining friends as Billy B, laughed beside him and patted Jim's rifle barrel. "He means it." Billy spit some of his last Red Man chaw on the dirt before him.

The man and the woman immediately put their hands in the air.

Billy only noticed the woman. Despite the dirt and blood caked in her long, unkempt hair and across her gray shirt, she was a looker.

The man slowly stepped forward. "We're in trouble and we need help."

"Shit, we all in trouble here, boy," Jim said and leveled the rifle at the man's head. "Why don't you turn around and go back the way you come?"

"Pembroke is overrun, as well as most of Giles County."

"Giles County?" Billy asked. Jim poked him in the chest with the rifle butt.

The man looked confused. "My name is Eric Fries. My wife and I – this is Mary - were hiking this part of the Appalachian Trail when all Hell broke loose."

"What's going on?" Billy asked, rubbing his chest.

"The dead are eating people," the woman said with a wild look in her eyes. "Just tearing into people, right before your eyes." She put her hands on her head and began crying.

"Shut her up or I swear I'll pull this damn trigger," Jim said.

Eric nodded. "Look, we're all scared, but we're on the same side. We're alive and those things are slowly moving up the trail. They can't be more than ten minutes behind us."

"I don't care. You need to turn it around." Jim didn't have time to argue, he needed these stupid people to not move another step in his direction.

"Let them go around us, Jim. I told you that something crazy was going on but you wouldn't listen."

The Remington was a heavy weapon, and when Jim brought it across his partner's face everyone could hear his jaw pop. "I told you yesterday not to question me, and we'd get out of this." He glanced at the couple. "Now I'll have to kill them."

"No need for that. If we could just move past you, we'll be gone. I don't think you understand what's going on. The dead are biting people and turning them into undead."

"That doesn't make sense," Jim said.

"It doesn't but it's true. Unless you've been in these woods for the last three days you've heard about what's going on," Eric said. He looked frantic now, glancing back the way they'd come.

"Sorry, but we're Appalachian proper folk. We live out here, and this is our land. We don't take kindly to trespassing Yankees," Jim said.

"You're more of a Yankee than I am," Eric said with annoyance in his voice. "You keep trying for the fake accent but I hear New England in your words. Who are you trying to kid? You might be wearing dusty clothes and trucker caps on backwards, and you haven't shaved in days, but I can smell the hotel soap from here and see your dress shoes."

Jim shot Eric in his left leg just above the kneecap.

Mary screamed and fell onto her husband when he hit the ground, the blood spraying in all directions. In seconds she was covered, her cries echoing through the silent woods.

Billy B., his face shattered, stood on buckling legs and pulled his hunting knife.

Jim laughed and put the nasty end of the Remington squarely on his partner's forehead. "Finally got some balls, Billy? After weeks on the run, you finally grow a pair?"

"Pull that trigger if you want, Jim, because we're already dead."

"How poetic." Jim licked his lips. "We need to get out of here."

"What about them?"

"What about them? If the world is coming to an end and dead people are killing living people, it's time we did what we always did well: fend for ourselves, take what we can and survive like we always do."

"What you did to that woman back there was awful," Billy said in a whisper. "There was no need for that." Billy rubbed his jaw, which he was sure was broken. It hurt to even talk.

"There's always a need for that." Jim pointed the rifle at the sky and looked at Mary, still crying over Eric. "Maybe it's finally Billy's turn, eh? I know you were looking at her."

Billy looked away. "The stealing isn't a problem for me, and you know it. But this," Billy pointed at the woman and then pointed behind them," and back there… I didn't sign up for that."

"You knew me, right? Knew what I was more than capable of. Did you think the stories I told you in the joint were lies? I like to have some fun with my whores, and the more they fight back the more I like them."

"Not me."

Mary was wailing now.

Jim shrugged. "To each his own, right? If you don't want this one I'll gladly have her. She'd cute."

Mary suddenly stopped screaming and the silence was deafening. Both men turned and stared, stunned, by the sight before them.

While they had chatted four people had come up silently and two of them clamped down on Mary's neck and arms with gore-crusted teeth.

"Holy, Holy Mother of God…" Billy said and felt his bowels release.

Jim raised the rifle and pulled the trigger but nothing happened.

Billy, his fear overriding the pain from his face, turned and ran.

"Damn gun!" Jim yelled behind him.

Serves him right. He probably busted it when he hit me in the face with it, Billy thought. Regardless, he wasn't going to wait around to see if he could fix it.

Two shots rang out behind him and Billy ran faster, trying to keep to the trail in front of him.

When he tripped over the body of the mutilated woman and flew through the air, he almost laughed at the irony of the situation. *It's like she tripped me,* he thought before a new, horrific pain exploded in his face as he hit the dirt and screamed in pain.

He heard another shot behind him, close, before Jim leapt over his body.

"Partner?" Billy croaked through shattered teeth. "Help?"

Jim disappeared around the bend, dust swirls kicking up behind him.

Billy didn't have to look when he heard the shuffling coming up behind him. he closed his eyes and prayed that the pain he was experiencing now would be enough to knock him out before the real hurt began.

Swim Out Past The Breakers

Mike paddled north, past the lighthouse, but the dead still paced with him. He could see dozens of them on the beach while Florida burned behind them.

Now he would have kicked himself in the ass if he could. He'd ignored the protests of Jennie to stay with her today and watch the local news to see what was happening. Instead, he'd called out from his dead-end job and hit the waves. It wasn't often you got a free pass to surf instead of work, right?

When New Smyrna began to burn it was too late. Mike had been out here for at least three hours, paddling and riding and lost in his thoughts. The faint smell of smoke smacked him back to reality. Was someone cooking on the beach? It was the town that he'd been born and raised in that was cooking.

As he'd paddled into the breakers the first undead had shown up over the dunes, three more shambling behind it. Mike, even at this distance, knew something was wrong. Seriously wrong. He decided to swim north with his board and get into Daytona Beach and try to get home.

But they'd swarmed slowly over the dunes and beach accesses. Mike could only watch as beachgoers and tanners were summarily bitten – and worse – under the sun, blood and gore staining the sand.

His legs and arms ached from fighting the current. His progress was too slow and he watched as more and more ventured to join the crowd and watch and wait for him.

Mike decided that he'd rather drown out here than be brutalized by these things.

As the sun dropped and his body, burnt and waterlogged, tried to keep moving, Mike was terrified. He could see the many figures still on the beach because of the raging fires behind them. He knew that Daytona Beach and farther north were aflame. There would be no escaping to land.

Something brushed against his bloated leg. At first he ignored it. He smelled the blood before he felt it. Panicking, he slipped off of his board and bumped into something below him in the water. His legs had cramped and he fought to grip the surfboard with swollen fingers but failed.

He suddenly wondered if Jennie was on the beach. His blood, black and slick in the moonlight and glow from the shore, circled him. Mike closed his eyes and waited for the inevitable.

Blind In Texas

The blast threw Billy Rice clear off the oil rig, snapping his harness with such force that it shot a hundred feet in the opposite direction and depositing him inside the ditch that the men affectionately called The Piss Pit.

Hours later, in the dark, Billy pulled himself from the ditch reeking of piss and blood, his left arm broken and both kneecaps undoubtedly fractured or at least damn-well bruised.

He didn't know the time but guessed it was somewhere around three in the morning, because it was pitch black. It must be cloudy tonight because he lifted his face and didn't see the stars above.

Billy Rice didn't see his good right hand when he moved it across his face. He panicked, slapping at his eyes. He couldn't see. *I'm blind, I'm fucking blind,* he screamed in his head. The blast must have taken his sight somehow, maybe the shock or the damage to his body had done it. He felt his face but didn't feel anything broken or loose or bleeding. Billy was definitely not one hundred percent, but he was still alive. He could still smell, and he knew the rig was aflame and spewing oil and ash into the air. He could feel the sand under his body and knew that he could crawl to the parking lot from here. He could hear… what did he hear?

"Billy…"

The whisper so close to his ear startled him and he screamed as he rolled away. Someone tackled him, someone large, and put a rough hand over his mouth.

"Shut up, you fucking idiot. There's two of them in the parking lot and Brad Gentry just took a chunk out of Allyson's fucking tit."

Billy moved the hand from his mouth. "Who's there?"

"What? Shit, what the fuck are you staring at? It's me. Mack."

"Mack, I'm blind. I can't see a damn thing right now."

"Shit. We need to get you to a hospital. Can you walk?"

"I don't know. My arm is broken and I think I screwed up both legs. What's going on? One second I was running a line and the next I was in The Piss Pit."

"Yeah, you smell awful." Mack finally got off Billy. "I hope they can't smell."

"Who?"

"Who? Fuck! How long you been out? The fucking world is ending right before your eyes… shit, sorry about that, it's just a figure of speech."

"It's alright. I'm not permanently blind," Billy whispered. *God, you hear me? I'm not permanently blind.* "Tell me what's going on. Please."

"We were all up on platform two, fixing to take a fifteen as soon as Gentry came up and made the call as usual. He came up, but he looked like shit. At first Marlin Simmons snorted at him – you know how he does that stupid snort thing when he's laughing? – and asked if he'd fallen off the wagon. Now, you know the problems with the sauce that Gentry has had in his time, so we didn't think it was funny. Besides, Marlin is nothing short of an asshole. Still… when Gentry grabbed him by the arm and bit him we thought even he'd gone too far. That's when all Hell broke loose."

"He actually bit him?" Billy said.

"Yeah, blood everywhere. It was pretty fucked up. A couple of guys, not sure who now, tried to subdue him but in short order they were gushing blood from neck wounds. Guys were trying to get off of the rig, but Gentry was blocking the way."

"That's crazy. What got over him?"

"Who knows? What was really fucked up is that Marlin and a couple other guys stood up, with the same fucked-up look in their eyes as Brad, and they started tearing and biting everyone on the platform. We had no choice but to go up. I thought about jumping."

"I was up on six."

"We got to four, but guys were getting bit behind us and then joining in."

"That's crazy."

"That's not the worst part, Billy." Mack was real close to Billy again and Billy winced at the sour breath pummeling him. "Donald Lewis was up there but we ran right past him. Marlin and those others just, well, they just…"

"They just what?"

"They fucked him."

"They killed him? They bit him?"

"No, you don't understand." Mack paused and Billy didn't know if he was going to finish his thought. Just when he was about to question him Mack started talking again, this time in a whisper and with something new in his voice. Fear?

"They literally fucked him. They ripped his clothes off and raped him until he died."

Billy felt his stomach churning.

"A minute later the top of the rig exploded and everyone up top was thrown and killed."

"Not everyone."

"No, but you'll probably wish you'd been killed by the end of this shit-storm. We need to get out of here. They're all around us."

"I can't see," Billy said a bit too loudly.

"Shh... fuck, Allyson just started moving towards us. Her sweet Jesus tits are all bloody and torn open. Shit."

"Then we need to get around her and get to your truck."

"My truck is on fire right now. The damn platforms slammed into and destroyed half the parking lot." Mack grunted. "She's heading our way and there's two more behind her now. Shit."

"What about my truck?"

"Where'd you park?"

Billy thought about it. "I parked near the main gate because I was almost late this morning."

"Then you should still be fine. Of course, that means we have a lot of goddamned ground to cover and you aren't exactly going to be helpful trying to elude these fuckers."

Billy smiled. "Can you do me a favor, Mack?"

"Sure, buddy, anything."

"Stop using profanity and taking the Lord's name in vain."

"Fuck yeah I will, Godamnit. Anything for you, Ray Charles."

"I'm glad you're getting a laugh at all of this."

"I pissed myself twice as we sat here. I'm scared shitless, Billy."

"Just let me know what I need to do."

Billy felt Mack's hand on his shoulder. "We're going to get up and run like Hell. I'll keep a grip on you and let you know which way to turn."

"I think I can handle that." Billy sighed. "I'm still seeing nothing but I've been coming to this darn place for so long I can still picture the layout in my mind."

"I hope so. Let's get up slowly."

Billy tried to stand and immediately felt his legs burning. His head swam and he felt his stomach churning. He dropped to the ground, hitting both knees on the dirt. Hot tears poured from unseeing eyes and he vomited.

"Shut the fuck up, Billy, or I'm leaving you here."

"Huh?" Billy managed, covering his ears because a sound like a warped siren wouldn't stop.

When Mack shook him he realized that he had been making the noise, the bleating screams of pain burning his throat.

He felt a sharp slap across his face and smelled Mack's breath again, his nose touching his. "I swear to fucking God, Billy, you're drawing way too much attention. Either you shut your mouth or I leave you to die here. Got it?"

"Got it," Billy managed to say. His jaw stung and he could taste his own blood from a cut lip. "You hit hard, Mack."

"No shit. Now get up."

"I don't think I can."

Mack pulled Billy to a standing position slowly, his full weight draped over Mack. For a second Billy wanted to protest out of some macho code thing, but decided against it. What good would it do? Mack would either save him or leave him.

"I'm going to fireman's carry your ass to the parking lot and we're going to get to your truck. I need you to shut your mouth and not draw any attention, no matter what you hear."

"Got it." Billy felt himself being draped over Mack's shoulders. Despite his size, Mack seemed to be comfortable enough carrying him. He knew it was probably out of fear and desperation. Either way, he was glad that Mack found a reserve of strength to carry his fat ass out of this. *I swear, Lord, if you let me live through this, that starting tomorrow I will go on a diet and get to church more often than holidays.*

"Thanks, Mack," Billy whispered close to what he figured was his friend's ear.

"Shut up," Mack whispered back but even blinded Billy could hear the amusement in the statement. "If you try to kiss me I'll drop you."

"No problem." Billy tried to ignore the lingering pain from his throbbing knees.

"Fuck."

Billy felt Mack tense up underneath him and he stopped suddenly. Billy resisted the urge to ask questions, knowing that it probably wasn't prudent to be distracting his savior right about now. *I put my trust in your hands, Lord, and your humble blaspheming servant Mack.*

Billy was almost thrown when Mack made a sudden move to the left. Mack started moving quickly in that general direction and Billy almost made the mistake of asking aloud how close they were to the truck.

Mack's work boots clearly slapped against the asphalt of the parking lot and Billy smiled, even though it was still a long way to safety. He unconsciously rubbed his eyes, as if they were merely covered in dirt.

Suddenly Billy was floating in the air, his body no longer touching Mack. Before he could scream or flail in panic he slammed hard against the blacktop.

"Damn!" Billy shouted, pain exploding up his right side where he'd made contact. He was positive that his forearm was now broken, adding to the dulled pain from his initial fall. He tried to rise but his body fought him. Even without sight his head was swimming and he knew he was blacking out. He put his head down on the hot asphalt and closed his unseeing eyes, idly wondering if someone had spilled lukewarm water near his head.

It smelled like blood and filled his nostrils. He didn't know if he wretched before he finally passed out.

"Wake the fuck up, Billy. Jesus Christ you are heavy as a bag of shit."

The pain was so intense that Billy almost bit through his tongue, especially when Mack dragged-pulled-carried him across the hot ground.

"Sorry, buddy, but I can't hold them fuckers off any longer." Mack got a good grip around Billy's waist and lifted him onto one shoulder. "You're dead weight."

"Was that a pun?" Billy said between clenched teeth. His head was spinning and grey shapes swam before his ruined eyes.

Grey shapes?

"I think my eyes are adjusting back or something." Billy felt the sweat dripping from his face and… something else. "Am I bleeding?" he finally asked.

"For the last time, shut up. Every time you open your mouth five of them turn in our direction. I can't outpace them with you on my back. Literally."

Billy went to apologize and stopped himself again. He just needed to shut up, pray, keep the bile down in his stomach and hope that his eyesight returned. A large part of him didn't know if he wanted to see what was going on around him.

"Did we pass Brad Gentry's pickup just now?" Billy had to ask. The smell of dozens of those little trees attached to his rearview mirror always made Billy gag when he had to pass his truck on his way to the rig in the morning. He'd know that smell anywhere.

"Yes. Once again…"

"Yep, sorry." Billy felt some hope, the proverbial light at the end of the tunnel, because he knew that Gentry had parked two rows away from his truck and almost in a straight line. *We're almost there, almost in the clear.*

He heard a shuffling sound near his head and Mack yanked him roughly in the opposite direction. Something cold touched his face and he flinched but it was gone before he could bring a hand up for defense. *I'm useless without my vision. I'm such a burden for poor Mack. I'm going to get him killed out here.*

Mack was grunting heavily, and Billy felt his friend's muscles straining as he lugged him one step at a time.

"Almost there," he heard Mack mutter, figuring he was talking to himself. "Shit. I'm putting you down for a second."

Billy hit the ground ass-first and instinctively rolled up into the fetal position as he heard Mack struggling with someone or something. A string of profanity escaped his friend's lips and something fell close to Billy. He knew from the sound that Mack was kicking, his work boots meeting flesh.

"Time to go. We're at your truck. Where's the keys?"

"Keys?" Billy asked stupidly.

Mack was in his face again, pulling him up and leaning him against the cool vehicle. "Keys, man, your fucking car keys." Without waiting for an answer Mack was going through Billy's pockets, finding them and pulling them free. "I'll drive," Mack said.

The car door was unlocked and Billy was unceremoniously pushed onto the passenger seat. It smelled like home to him right now: rotting bits of cheeseburgers, spilled coffee, cigarettes and dirt.

Mack locked the door and slammed it shut.

Billy slipped down to the floorboards as best as he could; he was scared and didn't know what else to do. He couldn't feel his legs at all and feared that even if he lived through this he might need to have one or both amputated. He couldn't remember what he'd once read about losing blood circulation before having to cut off a limb. He thought he was already there.

Where was Mack? He didn't want to risk trying to get up on the seat. He didn't know if he could, anyway. Billy put his ear to the door.

Nothing. No sound.

Billy didn't know if it was deathly quiet out there or he just couldn't hear a thing. Either way he decided not to make a sound, move a muscle or breathe.

When the driver's side door was suddenly yanked open Billy yelped and covered his face.

"Shut up, you wimp," Mack said and laughed. "Don't worry, I'll do all of the work and you just lay there smelling like piss."

Billy laughed and tried to get up onto the seat but he was too weak.

The engine started and Mack jammed on the accelerator. Billy could sense the rocks shooting up behind them and the cloud of dust.

"Get up on the seat and enjoy this great escape with me," Mack yelled.

"I can't move my legs."

"I'll pull over once we clear this shit. I can't believe any of this."

"What's going on out there? Is it confined to the yard?" Billy asked.

"Hell no. The fucking town seems to be one big cluster-fuck of violence. The friggin' diner is burning and I swear we just passed Jennie, that waitress with the big tits, chomping on Officer Halliday. Always hated him, he gave me that speeding ticket in June because I was nine miles over the limit. But, still, that's a shitty way to die."

"Agreed." Billy tried to focus with his eyes, really concentrate. Maybe he could will them back to working. He knew it was better than it was because he could make out some dark gray shapes around the light gray shapes. Or maybe he was imagining it and hoping. Either way…

"Do you even want to know what's going on around us?" Mack asked as he cut the wheel sharply without warning and Billy slammed his head against the door.

"No," Billy hesitated. "Yes."

"Which is it?"

"Yes." Billy rubbed at his eyes again. The pain was one continuous pulse, his nerves raw and seething. It hurt to breathe deeply and even his teeth hurt, like they did when he was a kid and he got really sick from the flu.

"We're passing the gas station on the corner of Main and Clark."

"What's happening?" Billy got a vision like in the movies, with a jet of gas and flames shooting thirty feet into the air and cars scattering like leaves.

"Nothing. Can you believe gas is over four bucks today?"

Billy wanted to laugh but his head hurt. "You know what I'm asking."

"We pulled away from the immediate danger area, I guess. Everyone is running around in a panic as we hit near Wasserman's General Store, running out with water and bags of chips."

"Bags of chips?"

Mack laughed. "I guess if I had to have a last meal before being ripped apart by monsters it would either be a bag of chips or some good beef jerky. Ever have any of the beef jerky at Auntie Kim's restaurant? I love the teriyaki."

Billy knew that Mack was talking nervously now and the pickup truck sped up as he spoke. He decided to chit-chat with his friend to keep him calm. He decided he didn't want to know what was going on outside.

"Shit." Mack slowed down but didn't stop. Billy could feel the pickup bucking as Mack let off the gas and let it roll. "The little bridge over the creek is jammed with traffic. I might need to turn around and go the other way."

"What other way?"

"Through the fields."

"The oil fields? Are you crazy?"

"I just might be." Mack laughed. "Besides, this ain't my piece of shit truck, now is it?"

Before Billy could think of a sarcastic comeback the truck lurched, front wheels and then back banging around as they left the pavement and hit the sidewalk.

"I'll just take the scenic route around the Burger Palace and then cut through the Gibson Garage lot," Mack said.

"There's a fence there."

As the truck rocked again, throwing Billy's head back to slam on the dashboard, Mack whooped. "What fence?"

"I swear, if you dented my hood… I just got it painted," Billy managed, trying to joke and fight through the throbbing pain in his head. He decided that he'd close his worthless eyes and put his head down on the seat before him and pray that he'd wake soon.

"Stay with me, buddy," Mack said as Billy felt a smack on the side of his head, enough to jar him back awake.

"I think I'm going to puke."

"Not in my truck," Mack said. "Oh, wait, it's your truck."

Billy promptly vomited all over the seat and he felt it sliding down his shirt. He closed his eyes again and decided to will himself to pass out. Maybe he'd choke on his own vomit like some rock star and not get eaten.

* * * * *

Sunlight.

Billy felt it on his face but when he opened his eyes it was a sickly yellow streak before him. He lifted an unfeeling hand before his face and could make out his fingers if he strained.

His body was numb. The truck smelled of vomit, urine and blood.

"Mack?" he finally whispered through dry lips.

The air inside the truck was stifling. He shook his hands slowly to get circulation back, needles and pins shooting up his arm. The minor pain felt good when compared to the wracking pain that had destroyed his body.

Billy reached up and after what seemed like forever he touched the glass of the window. *Of course it's closed. What did you expect?*

He felt alone and wanted to cry, which almost made him laugh. *Pull yourself together, you're a grown man. Crying like a baby? Really?*

He decided to stay where he was, keep quiet, and eventually his eyesight would return. For the first time in a long time he thought of his children, all grown up and gone off to different parts of Texas with their own families, and he couldn't remember the last time he'd spoken to any of them.

"Once this is over I swear, Lord, that I'll make the time to drive to Dallas and see the grandkids and Billy Junior. Arlington ain't that far. Diana will be surprised to see her old man," he whispered to himself. He decided to turn over a new leaf. He'd never been a bad man but the years had slipped away from him and he'd neglected his duties as a father and grandfather.

He folded his shaking hands and bowed his head. "Lord, give me strength to get through this so that I can continue to do your work and help my children."

Something banged against the passenger door next to him.

Billy closed his eyes and put his hands close to his face.

The window above him shattered, spraying the top of his head with shards of glass.

"Amen," Billy whispered.

Caution, Smoke Ahead

Cheyenne Leone gripped the telephone with one hand and used the other to keep herself from not falling to the kitchen floor.

"Mom? It's me, Robin…"

This is impossible, there's no way after fifteen years she's on the other end of the line, Cheyenne thought. She sat down on one of the rickety chairs and put her scrawny elbows on the worn kitchen table, pushing dirty plates and a half-eaten potato chip out of her way. She realized that she was holding her breath and exhaled. "Robin?"

"Mom."

A thousand questions filled her head and she struggled to find the first one to open the floodgates. *Fifteen years.*

"It's daddy… I think he's dead."

Cheyenne closed her eyes, feeling the anger welling up inside of her. "Your daddy took you away from me."

"I know. Look, I need your help. He needs your help."

"How can I help a dead man?" Cheyenne knew that she'd said that with a bit of venom, and knew that she was glad that the bastard was dead. He'd stolen her little girl, run off with her cousin and called the cops on her and the heroin stashed in the closet. His stash.

"Mom, I'm scared."

"Why haven't you called me before now?" Cheyenne blurted. She felt like an asshole as soon as she said it, but she was now angry at her daughter as well. Fifteen years was a long time to wait before calling your mother, and then only when you were up shit's creek?

"I… daddy wouldn't let me. He told me you had a bad drug problem and gave me to him, he said you didn't care enough about me to keep in touch, and then he married Barbara and…"

"He couldn't have married someone else, because he was – is – still married to me, damnit. We never got a divorce, never got it annulled, and he stole you from me. Your daddy was the biggest heroin addict I knew. Shit, he got me hooked and in so deep that… I did things I'm not proud of, and I did them for that filthy sonofabitch. And in the end, he stole the only good thing in my life, got me put in jail and royally fucked me."

There was silence on the line and Cheyenne feared that Robin had hung up the phone. "Robin?"

"Mom, I'm scared," she repeated. "I don't know what to do."

Cheyenne put her head to the dirty table and clutched the phone. Her head was swimming and she closed her eyes. *My child is in need of her mother… forget the past; forget the hurt, just work on the Now.* "What happened?"

"Barbara came home from work and… I think they had a fight in the bedroom. I heard her screaming and making funny noises and then daddy was shouting and yelling for me to run."

"Do they fight often?" Cheyenne was trying to stay calm, even though thoughts of her younger second cousin Barbara fucking her husband made her clench the phone and squeeze her eyes shut. She resisted the urge to slam her head off of the table as well.

"Not really. Ever since daddy stopped the drinking he's been a decent man. He works a lot and so does Barbara. They are always happy and doing fun things. I've never seen them fight like that."

"What happened next?"

"I ran out the sliding doors into the yard and hid in the guest house on the other side of the pool."

"Pool?"

"Yes. We have an in-ground pool and I've kinda taken over the guest house for my own, since it has so much space. I hid in the walk-in closet."

"Sounds like you live pretty fancy." Cheyenne lifted her head and stared at the mildew at the corners of the kitchen floor and the scraps of food that hadn't been cleaned up. *Motherfucker has a pool now.*

"Mom, it's not about that right now."

"So, you're hiding in your guest house and you think Barbara killed him?"

"It looks like he was ripped apart."

"What did she use?" Cheyenne asked, her voice pitching higher. *Keep the personal out of this, your daughter needs you.* "Where was Barbara?"

"She was gone. It happened, like, six hours ago."

"Did you call the police?"

"No one answered 911 and… strange things are happening here."

"Like what?"

Robin sighed. "We're on a hill at the end of a cul de sac and the Romano's house – that's the one at the mouth of the street – is on fire."

"There's a fire? How close is it to you?"

"Seven houses down, but the properties are pretty wide. I smelled the smoke and thought it was our house."

"Do you think the fire has anything to do with your dad?"

"I don't know. None of the neighbors seem to be home, or else they're hiding. A police chopper came right over the house fifteen minutes ago and I can hear sirens in the distance."

"Where exactly are you?"

"Melbourne, Florida."

It was like a kick in the teeth to Cheyenne. "That motherfucker moved two hours away from me? All this time I'm trying to find him back in Virginia but his family is swearing he is long gone."

"Mom?"

"Shit." Cheyenne swept her arm across the table, jostling rotting food and debris onto the filthy floor. She realized she was losing it but right now she didn't care. "He didn't even have the balls to move out of state, go hide at the other end of the country or put some distance between us. That bastard stole my daughter, fell for that slut cousin of mine and then built some perfect fucking life, and left me here to rot?"

"Mom," Robin snarled. "This isn't about you right now. It's about me, trapped in a fucking house with a dead father and the neighborhood in flames. Jesus Christ."

Cheyenne smiled. *Like mother like daughter.* "Fair enough, baby." Cheyenne rose and searched for the keys to her sleeping boyfriend's piece of shit Nova.

* * * * *

I-95 was packed, cars cramming the north and south lanes and the medians. Cheyenne didn't hesitate; she stepped on the gas, the Nova bucking and puffing black smoke from its rear.

She ignored the people walking as she steered through the maze, beeping her horn and screaming back, waving her middle finger. The nice people, the ones who obeyed the laws in this lawless stretch of Florida, were suckers left for dead.

"I ain't a sucker," Cheyenne yelled, nearly clipping an old woman as she sped by at thirty miles an hour, the car bouncing and bottoming out over the median. It wasn't her car, and she would be damned if she'd worry about it. She had no intention of going back to that life or that fucking string of loser boyfriends or any of it. Her baby had called and was in trouble. "Thank you, Lord, for this gift," she said quietly as she cut the wheel and clipped a pickup truck before blowing past.

Cheyenne pounded the gas pedal and rode the grass for another half mile before the traffic moved to the right, hundreds of cars cramming to get off I-95 and exit to New Smyrna Beach. More than likely the roads there were jammed as well. She didn't know what was happening and didn't care; all she cared about was her daughter.

With regular traffic it would take her another hour to get to Melbourne, but she had no idea what she was going to run into.

Of course the radio didn't work in this pile of crap, so she couldn't hear news reports or traffic updates. She'd just have to run blind south and try to reach Robin.

Cheyenne had never been to Melbourne. She'd never been farther south than Daytona Beach, but figured it was just another beach town filled with jerk-off tourists, uppity locals and dickhead cops. She hoped to steer clear of all three groups.

Her hands were twitching and she knew what that meant. She needed a fix, but in her haste to rescue Robin she'd forgotten to rip off her boyfriend and grab his stash or his money. She didn't bother checking her pocketbook for money or drugs.

Maybe in the car?

Without another thought she pulled off the highway, even though there were no cars in the immediate area. She didn't want the risk of some maniac driver barreling down on her while she was rummaging.

Ten frantic minutes later she found a roach under the seat, wedged in between a fast food bag and what looked to be a desiccated piece of dog shit. She didn't care, as long as she could smoke the minute joint and get even a slight buzz.

"Motherfucker," she cursed when she pushed in the cigarette lighter in the Nova and it didn't work. "That figures." On her search no lighter had been found.

She was wasting too much time but she needed something to get her edge back and to get her head on straight. *Robin will understand*, she thought. She hoped.

Back on the highway she stamped down on the gas and was hitting ninety, the car rocking and bucking. Cheyenne hoped the Nova didn't fall apart before she got to Melbourne. The next exit was again jam-packed with cars trying to get off the road. A pull to the right and she was airborne and scraping the underside on the shoulder, sure that parts had fallen off like in a cartoon.

Cheyenne took the Melbourne exit at sixty, bumping an RV and sure that she'd hit a person, but she didn't tap the brakes. To her that person wasn't as important as her daughter.

The light signals were out and she ran through the intersection, ignoring horns beeping and brakes being slammed in her wake. She only had a vague idea of where she was going and didn't think it smart to stop and ask for directions. Something was definitely going on, something fucked up and big and scary and she didn't care as long as she could get to Robin.

And then, suddenly, she was at the right address and sitting in the stolen car, looking at a gorgeous house at the end of a block she could never afford. With the adjacent houses on fire, she knew she didn't have much time.

Cheyenne got out, fixed her hair with her hands in the side mirror, and walked up the driveway to reacquaint herself with her daughter.

* * * *

"Robin?" Cheyenne called out. The front door had been smashed apart and she stepped over the two halves of the door and into an entry hall.

Bile rose in her throat at the sight of the multitude of family photos displayed on the walls and an ornate table. Here was her husband, skinny, healthy, with shiny eyes and a warm smile Cheyenne had never seen. Her cousin Barbara was still a knockout, with golden blonde hair and a great body. Even in these pictures she was better than Cheyenne could ever be.

Cheyenne picked up a framed photo of the pair skiing and laughing. She dropped it to the ground with a satisfying explosion.

The pictures of Robin were difficult to look at. The left wall of the hallway was filled with a running story of her growth, from small child to young adult. She was striking with her father's eyes but her mother's cheekbones.

"A beautiful woman," Cheyenne whispered and touched a few of the pictures lightly, as if to feel them would force them to shatter like crystal. This was the daughter she never knew and could never know; the happiness and the pain she could never experience.

She focused on a picture of Robin in pigtails, in her soccer uniform, holding a giant trophy and smiling. Her two front teeth were missing.

Cheyenne should have been there when those teeth fell out, and watched Robin place them under her pillow and ask the tooth fairy for money. She should have been there for so many key moments in her daughter's life, but he'd taken it away from her.

She turned away, choking back a sob, and stared directly into a full-length mirror on the bathroom door. Her initial reaction was shock before realizing it was her she was looking at.

"You look like shit," she admitted aloud. *When was the last time you hadn't?* Her makeup was smeared down her face, her lipstick blood-red and tacky. The wrinkles around her eyes and mouth were like canyons, the extra skin dripping off her neck. Her skin was gray and unhealthy. Cheyenne could still feel the scant traces of drugs coursing through her veins, the smell of alcohol and vomit on her clothes. She was a mess, a burnt-out druggie who looked fifteen years older than she was.

A groan down the hall brought her back to reality, as shitty as reality was for her. She wanted to kick herself for standing here, wasting time, while her helpless daughter was trapped somewhere in this house.

This big, beautiful house.

The living room was open, with creamy leather couches and a widescreen television set into one wall. Cheyenne realized the fish tank, back-lit and huge, was worth more than her home. And she didn't even own that.

She felt like an intruder, like those crack whores you see on the news doing a home invasion with their drugged-out boyfriend. Every brain impulse was begging her to run out the front door, get back in the stolen car, and get back to her crappy life.

The moan was coming from down the hall, and she moved, her daughter the only care she had now.

"Robin?" she asked at the nearest closed door. "Honey, are you in there?"

The knock came from down the hall and scared her in the silence of the house.

Cheyenne went to the last door on the left and tried the doorknob. Locked. "Robin, honey, are you hurt?"

Something moved inside, the sound of clothes moving or something vaguely familiar to Cheyenne.

"Step away from the door, I'm going to break it down," she said and took two steps away. When she ran back into it, leading with her shoulder, she was ready for the explosion of wood like in the movies, but instead it felt like her arm had exploded.

As if in answer she heard another moan from the other side of the door, low and guttural. Robin was in pain, and Cheyenne picked herself up slowly and rubbed her arm, but she knew she had to get to her daughter.

She kicked at the door and it shook but didn't open, so she took a step back and kicked with all her might. The door burst open and slammed into Barbara, who shot across the room and fell heavily onto the bed.

Cheyenne's initial reaction was to apologize and help her cousin up, but then the anger rose in her. This was the bitch who'd stolen her husband, who'd gone against family and helped steal her baby.

"I hope that hurt, you fucking bitch," Cheyenne finally spat. She balled her fists and was about to punch Barbara out when Barbara stood stiffly. Her eyes were bloodshot, her face covered in blood and peeling flesh.

"What the Hell?" Cheyenne whispered. Before she could move Barbara raised her arms and charged her, closing the gap between them in two jerky strides.

Barbara clamped cold, broken fingers on Cheyenne's neck and squeezed.

Cheyenne was overcome with such hatred toward Barbara that her emotions took control. She punched the hands away from her and slammed her forehead into her cousin's face, attempting to drive her back and hopefully break her nose. Cheyenne wasn't above fighting dirty; in fact, she always fought with anything she could get her hands on. She remembered the time she'd hit her husband with the ashtray because he smoked the last joint.

Thinking about him again got her swinging but Barbara wasn't even fazed, even though her nose was in ruins. Cheyenne was infuriated that her head-butt hadn't dropped the bitch. In fact, she didn't look stunned at all. She looked... *dead?*

A quick check of the room and Cheyenne noticed the ornate metal chairs surrounding a matching table with a shattered glass mirror mounted to its top. She grabbed one of the chairs and swung wild, connecting with Barbara's face and doing more damage. Amazingly Barbara started to rise from where she'd fallen to the floor, but Cheyenne had had enough. She began slamming the chair into her cousin until it was a twisted pretzel of metal in her hands.

Barbara had finally stopped moving.

* * * * *

"The guest house," Cheyenne remembered, trying to catch her breath and grabbing the unbroken metal chair. She was hoping her husband was still here but alive so he could feel every brutal smash against his face.

She didn't know what had happened to Barbara and she didn't dwell on it. The bedroom had thick velvet drapes covering one wall and when she pulled them away she gasped. The sliding glass door was ajar, and without the curtains blocking a thick gray smoke began pouring into the room.

Cheyenne pulled off her dirty shirt and covered her mouth and nose, moving into the yard and hoping for fresh air.

She took a few steps, her eyes burning, and then her right foot was suddenly in mid-air. She tripped forward and fell into the swimming pool, water shooting up her nose and down her throat. She struggled to break the surface, but her eyes burned from the smoke and then the chlorine in the pool, and she was blinded.

I can't die here, not like this, not so close to seeing my daughter again, her mind screamed as she squirmed and thrashed in the water. She couldn't help her body trying to breathe and gulped more water down her throat.

Suddenly she felt a strong grip on her head, fingers wrapping around her hair. She was yanked up and out of the water, air bursting into her lungs. She was slammed against the side of the pool, her upper torso out of the water.

"Sonofabitch," she coughed, a trickle of water dribbling down her chin. Her husband, eyes rimmed with blood, had her by the hair and stood over her.

Without a thought she grabbed his lead foot and pulled at him. He tipped and she used his momentum against him to force him over her and into the water.

He didn't let go, however, and she nearly blacked out when his grip held and she went back under. In a panic she began struggling, but she could feel the hair being pulled out by the roots and imagined her blood mixing in the pool water.

It was all too much for her and she gave up, doing her best to swallow as much water as she could and drown herself before her husband actually killed her.

Her only regret in life was not seeing her daughter again.

As she felt his grip loosen on her head and her body drifting away, she had to laugh to herself. Only regret? Fuck, her entire life was one regret after another. She'd never believed in blaming others for her mistakes, although it was her parents who fucked her royally before divorcing when she was two, or the uncles that molested her, or the teachers that ridiculed her, or the high school counselor that she was abused by, or the drugs and alcohol that so many men in her life made her dependent on...

And this dick-head totally screwed her, hooking her on the hard stuff and taking her baby from her. Not to mention running off with her slut cousin.

"Mom, is that really you?"

Cheyenne began coughing, water burning her throat as she spit up. She was dead and in hell, her daughter's voice forever haunting her. She refused to open her eyes.

Hands shook her and Cheyenne reluctantly opened her bruised eyes, the smoke so thick they began to water.

She was dragged on the coping of the pool and across the cement before regaining some composure to fight back. She figured this bastard was now going to bury her somewhere in the yard or toss her into the fire.

Instead, she was pulled into a house and the door closed, scattering the smoke.

"Mom?"

Cheyenne opened her eyes fully and laughed, alternately choking on the water and the smoke. Before her was Robin, her long-lost daughter, the only reason she was still alive. "You saved me," Cheyenne croaked and then coughed up water.

Robin hugged her, and the grip gave Cheyenne strength. She started to cry and squeezed her daughter as close to her as she could.

"We need to leave, he'll be coming," Robin whispered. "I only knocked him into the pool, but he's… he's not right."

"He was never right, especially with all the shit he put me through. I missed you so much. I can't believe it's really you."

Robin stood and held her arm, which was covered in blood and a pus-filled wound. "We need to go."

"What happened to your arm, baby?" Cheyenne asked, motherly instinct taking over. She reached a hand out but hesitated, not wanting to touch the vile gash. It looked infected, black and blue bruising spreading over her skin as she watched.

"Daddy bit me, but we need to move," Robin said.

"I parked outside," Cheyenne said.

There was a sudden bang on the door and both women jumped.

"It's daddy," Robin said and looked around. "We need something to kill him with."

"I had a metal chair," Cheyenne said. "I killed Barbara with it." She paused when something heavy hit the door again. "But I think she was already dead."

"That doesn't make sense," Robin said.

"She had this crazy, dead look on her face, really weird. She didn't even feel anything I did to her."

"Was she passed out?"

Cheyenne shook her head in answer and to clear her head. "She was… alive, but she wasn't. I don't know. I was too busy smashing her fucking head open with the chair to ask her if she was breathing. She just seemed so distant but was attacking me. Does that make sense?"

"None of this makes sense."

"We need the other chair. With it we can defeat him," Cheyenne said.

"It's at the bottom of the pool, mom."

Cheyenne didn't want to go anywhere near that pool again, sure that she had a fear of water after the attack.

"What are you smiling at?" Robin asked.

Cheyenne touched her lips. She was smiling. She looked up at her daughter. "You called me mom."

Robin stared at her with a blank expression on her face. "Let's get through this and out of here and then we can talk, alright?" Robin looked out the window and gasped.

The door shuddered.

"The houses on either side of us are on fire. We need to fight past him and escape before it's too late."

"How?"

"I guess we open the door and slam him with something." Robin looked around the room and settled on her lamp. She quickly unplugged it and stood near the door. "Open the door."

Cheyenne obeyed, unlocking and throwing it open.

There stood her husband, face and hands bloody, staggering in the doorway.

Robin wasted no time, swinging the lamp and connecting with her father in the head, but he didn't budge. She swung again but he moved in and closed the gap and her strike bounced harmlessly against his shoulder. His gore-stained fingers wrapped around her neck.

Cheyenne punched him square in the back but it had no effect. Robin pushed against him, managing to move outside but not releasing his grip.

Robin was turning a sickening color as her air was being shut off from her throat, and her struggles grew less and less.

Cheyenne reached between her husband's legs and grabbed his manhood, but he didn't wince. It was then she knew he was truly dead.

The smoke was so thick that her eyes stung again. She tried to find an object to kill him with but couldn't see more than a few feet in front of her.

"Hold your breath, baby," Cheyenne cried out to her daughter, who had closed her eyes and went limp. Her husband sunk his teeth into her neck.

Cheyenne tackled both of them, driving her husband into the pool with a splash. They went under and Cheyenne brushed against the metal chair on the bottom. She reached down, lifted it, and swam to the surface.

When her husband bobbed to the top she slammed him in the head three times, each blow caving in more of his head. Finally, he stopped moving and sunk into the pool, blood and brains drifting on the surface.

"Robin?"

Cheyenne had to close her eyes they hurt so much. She reached into the pool with her hands, kicking her feet until she found Robin underwater. Pulling her daughter up, she dragged-swam-crawled to the shallow end and to the steps.

She brushed the hair from her daughter's eyes and put a hand to her neck, where the blood was flowing. "Don't leave me, baby, not now. Mommy's here for you, everything will be alright. Mommy is here to save you."

Robin opened her swollen eyes, white and unseeing. She opened her mouth and blood trickled from her bottom lip.

"We'll be safe now, baby. I killed that sonofabitch. We can be together again, and make up for lost time."

Cheyenne couldn't help but smile as her daughter snuggled her neck and they hugged, even when her teeth sunk into the flesh of her shoulder.

This Is The End

"It's over, Harry! We've won! This is the end," the man shouted from the road in front of the compound.

Harry, unused to voices, was startled and almost dropped his rifle off of the roof of his house. He lifted his trusted weapon and looked through the sight.

Directly in front of the electrified chain-link fence, just in front of the gasoline-filled moat and in between the spiked rusty spears stood a man.

Harry had seen enough of the undead in the last three years, maneuvering in and out of his booby traps and tripwires, and rotting corpses as far down as the main road was testament to his defenses. Some of them still twitched after all these months.

Every day for the last three years he'd spent the bulk of his time on this roof, where he'd rigged a comfy seat, and a canopy for inclement weather. Food and drink were getting scarce, with only his small garden out back and boiled water from the rain gutters. The last of his pigs had been killed last winter. A week ago a deer had crashed through the defenses and been snagged on one of the bear traps. It looked sickly and Harry didn't want to take the chance that it was actually dead and infected. He'd slammed its head in with a rock.

"Damn, Harry! It's me, you ornery old coot! It's your brother Joe."

"Joe. Hmm," Harry said. He checked the sight again. It could be his brother Joe, although he hadn't seen him in five years. Before the apocalypse, before Harry decided to cut off the rest of the crazy world and fend for himself, he'd disowned his entire family. "You still owe me twenty dollars."

Harry could hear the familiar laugh of his brother. "Money ain't worth the paper it's written on, Harry."

"It's the point."

"I suppose it is." Harry watched as Joe shuffled from foot to foot and held his arms wide. "I'm inviting you to join us down at town hall. We've beaten them and are trying to get the town back in order. We'd love to have you with us."

"I'm fine right here." Even as Harry said it his stomach growled. He'd been eating asparagus for the past three days, even though he hated it. The rain hadn't come in over a week and he was down to about four gallons.

"I'm your brother, and I miss you. Let's forget about all of that past stuff and start again. The whole world is starting again."

Harry thought for a long moment as he clutched his rifle and peered at his brother Joe, shuffling on his heels.

When he pulled the trigger and shot him in the heart he was not surprised to see that Joe didn't fall down.

"It's a new world, Harry. I told you. Come join us. You're the last of your kind."

The second shot was a perfect headshot between the eyes. Joe fell down then.

Sanctuary

Keith tried to ignore Danny as he ate, checking the battery supply once again. In the twenty by thirty concrete bunker there wasn't much room to move and nowhere to be alone.

And the kid ate with his fucking mouth open like a horse. Keith glanced at Danny's mother, Irene, knowing better than to correct the little brat. *Shit, at thirteen, you should know proper table manners*, Keith thought. He went through the motions of counting ninety-eight size D battery packs, carefully putting them back in the marked cardboard boxes on the metal shelving.

When Keith turned back the first thing he noticed was the opened cereal box on the small table in the center of the room. Danny was sitting on his bedroll, listening to his iPod. Keith nearly lost it, but before he could explode Irene was in his face.

"Problem?" she asked with a challenge in her tone. "You've done nothing but harp on my kid since we got here."

Keith, trying to remain calm, pointed at the box of Count Chocula on the table. "That's the second box he's opened and left opened to spoil."

"So what? I brought eighteen boxes of cereal, and they'll probably go bad before we eat all of it anyway."

"That's not the point," Keith said. "Once these supplies are gone, we're fucked."

"Watch your language around my son."

Keith laughed. "You think he's never heard profanity before? Shit, he's thirteen. He probably knows more curses than I do."

"That's not the point," Irene countered. "We had definite rules before I agreed to come here with you." Without another word Irene turned away from him.

Keith turned back to counting his batteries and tried his best to ignore her. *Fucking bitch and her little pussy kid.* He wondered why he'd wasted his time and invited her. He glanced back as she was bending over the bedroll, talking softly to her kid, and saw the reason: she had such a great ass. For a woman in her late thirties she was hot, with a skinny little waist, nice big, juicy tits and that sweet butt. Stupidly, he thought he'd be tapping that pussy while the world ended around him. Now he was stuck with her attitude and her annoying brat.

He suddenly realized that Danny was watching him watch her ass move and he turned away, but he had to smile. *What are you going to do about it, punk?*

"It's time for the radio, Keith," she said quietly.

He glanced at his wristwatch and nodded. Every four hours they turned on the radios and listened for any news, anyone else alive, just any noise.

They found nothing but static for the fifth day in a row.

"Where'd everybody go?" Danny asked.

Keith shrugged his shoulders. "I'm not sure. We heard the last news together, so you know just as much as I do." He realized he had an edge to his voice when he said that and the dirty look from Irene meant she didn't miss it. She didn't miss a damn thing.

They turned the radios off and put them back on the shelf. Keith fingered through the dozens of paperback books he'd been collecting but nothing looked good right now. He decided on doing a crossword in one of the fifty puzzle books he'd amassed.

He glanced at Danny and Irene and sighed. Maybe later he'd make nice with them and start fresh, because he didn't think they'd find another living person out there with the radio.

* * * * *

"We're missing two packs of AA batteries," Keith said. He knew exactly where they went: into Danny's iPod, even though he didn't ask. Keith held up the torn packages and shook them. "And someone left the garbage in the run so they wouldn't be found."

"Seriously? Are they your batteries only?" Irene yelled.

"Keep your voice down."

"Why?" she screamed. "There's no one to hear me! It's been eighteen days without so much as a peep out there, total radio silence! The CB radio is static. We're the last people alive, don't you get it?"

The dull bang on the door brought them to silence.

Danny pulled his iPod headphones off and ran to his mother. "What was that?" he whispered.

Keith put his hand up and they all froze, but the sound was not repeated. Carefully Keith went to the locked gun closet and waited there, key in hand, for what seemed like hours.

Irene finally spoke. "Do you think it was a living person?"

Keith shrugged and noticed with disdain that Danny went to the foodstuffs and ripped open a box of Oreo cookies, destroying the wrapper so they wouldn't be able to close it. *Another waste of food*, Keith thought and tried not to scream.

"You should've put in some sort of window," Irene said.

And a swimming pool? Maybe an observation deck? An ice cream parlor? Keith put the key back in his pocket. "I only had three weeks to dig the hole, set the cement and blocks and stock it. I think I did a damn fine job before the world took a shit."

Irene scrunched her face. "Language."

Keith looked over at Danny, who was back on his bedroll but smiling at him. He wanted to punch the little bastard in the face.

"When are we going to open the door and see what's happening?" she asked.

"I don't think it's safe. Once we get anything on the radio, we'll figure that out. Not until then."

"Eighteen days," Irene said with a wave of her hand before going back to sit with her son.

* * * * *

"My question is simple, really: how much can he possibly eat each day?"

Irene balled her fists at her sides and pursed her lips.

Keith pointed at the mounting pile of folded cereal boxes and filled black garbage bags taking up a corner. "It's been twenty-eight days but, at this rate, we'll be out of food in five months instead of six."

"Your point?" she finally said with venom.

Keith closed his eyes and rubbed his eyes, which were starting to hurt from the unnatural light of the bunker. With only three lamps plugged into a power-strip, which in turn ran to the generator and two backup generators in the closed room on the other side of the east wall, all four corners were usually encased in darkness.

"Stop attacking my kid," Irene screamed.

Keith looked over at Danny, who was smiling and digging into a box of Munch-O's. Keith imagined his hands locked firmly around the boy's neck, squeezing the life out of him while the Munch-O's spilled from his mouth.

Irene pushed him, bringing him out of his fantasy. "Are you ignoring me again?"

"Don't touch me," Keith said quietly.

Irene backed up, fear etched in her face. For the first time she had nothing to say.

Keith wanted to choke her as well.

* * * * *

"Honey, slow down," Irene whispered to her son, but Keith heard her. How could he not? A good chunk of the bunker was now refuse, and the 'toilet' - a hole in the corner with a sheet tied up - had apparently filled and was going to back up soon.

Danny had dug into the last box of cereal, shoving handfuls into his mouth. He ignored his mother, stepping past her to grab yet another pack of batteries from the shelf.

"We have four packs of AA batteries left, and need them for one of the radios," Keith said.

"For what? There's no one out there, old man," Danny said and ripped open the packaging, tossing the debris on the floor.

Keith stared at Irene but she looked away.

"Danny, we need to slow down." Irene sat down on the floor next to her son, who folded into his bedroll again, changing the batteries of his iPod.

"For what? Once the food runs out we're screwed anyway. And it smells like shit in here," Danny said.

"Watch your language," Irene said.

Danny ignored her, standing up and staring at Keith. "What the hell are we waiting for, the dead to kick down the door and eat us?"

"We're waiting for a rescue team," Keith said but he had to look away when he said it. The chances of them being saved were less than zero. They'd had no communication, not even a noise outside in weeks. They were on their own.

Irene looked like she was about to cry. "Danny, he's right. We don't know what's out there. You saw how it was before Keith took us in."

Danny went back down on the bedroll and shifted away from them, burying his face in his pillow.

Keith felt something like pity. He was only a kid, no matter how annoying he was or how he got in the way, ate too much, used all the supplies, and got between the adults whenever Keith thought he might have a shot with Irene.

They separated, doing their own thing in such a cramped space.

Keith glanced at the door, but knew it would be wrong to venture out there. He had weapons; he'd made sure to pack his locker with every rifle and pistol he could purchase before the shit hit the fan. While his neighbors were laughing about the northern States being ransacked by the living dead, Keith had jumped into action. It was like he'd always known, and he'd been waiting for this his entire life.

At the first newscast about the craziness of people coming back to life and biting people and turning them, he'd simply stopped going to work, ordered a crew to dig and build the bunker, and went about amassing supplies.

Parents ignored his protests at the supermarket as he purchased every bottle of water, every last can of soup, and every battery he could find. He put it all on his credit card, knowing he'd never have to pay it back.

He boarded up his house after piling each room with extra supplies and then securing the rooms for possible use in the future, even when his neighbors laughed.

All but Irene, the new woman who'd just moved in across the street. For weeks he'd tried his best to talk to her, even though she was a few years younger, but she'd only been pleasant to him. Once everything started to roll and the bunker was being finished in the yard - and the stockade fence built surrounding his property, city be damned - she'd come over with a plate of cookies and a smile.

Keith knew now that it was desperation in her eyes that made her flirt just enough to get him to ask her to join him. He knew now that she'd been paying attention to the news and the internet but she'd started gathering items too little too late.

The crazy bastard across the street was the only viable option for her and her brat, he knew. Keith had planned it all out, with enough food and supplies to last him over a year, and comfortably.

This pretty mother - shit, if he was being honest, she was a damn MILF - had snowballed him into taking her and Danny in without a fight. Keith laughed to himself, because when she'd shown up with the cookies and enough cleavage to give a man a heart attack, she could've probably talked him into handing over the keys to the bunker and the house and the clothes on his back for a chance to see those boobs unleashed.

He was getting a hard-on again and turned away, making pretend he was doing a crossword puzzle, even though he'd finished them.

"Spent your whole life alone, and at the end of the world, just when you think you're finally getting laid..." he whispered.

"Did you say something?" Irene asked.

Keith just shook his head, not bothering to look at her and get his privates excited again.

* * * * *

"So, old man, you wanna bang my mom?"

Keith shot up from his bedroll, eyes useless in the pitch black of the bunker. "Huh?" was all he could manage.

Danny shined a flashlight in his eyes. "Be quiet or you'll wake my mom."

Keith sat up, blocking the light with his hands. "Get that out of my fucking face, kid." Now he really wanted to choke the shit out of him.

"I'm going outside. You with me?"

Keith stood, grateful that Danny lowered the beam of light to his feet. "No, are you nuts?"

"Who's the pussy?" Danny asked with a grin.

"You little bastard."

"Quiet." Danny turned his head slowly and pointed the flashlight. "We don't want to wake up mom, do we? What do you think she'd say?"

"About what?"

Danny made a big show rubbing his chin. "Oh, I don't know, let's see: mom wakes up, I scream and tell you to stop touching my dick, you sick old man pervert… what do you think she'll do? You'll never bang her then."

"Stop saying that." Keith was getting flustered and was still half-asleep. "No one is leaving."

"I am. I've had enough of this lying around, annoying you, and listening to the same fifty songs on shuffle. Since you're too chicken-shit to open the door and take a peek I'm going to go."

"That's insane."

"Insane is counting the same battery packs every day like clockwork. That's insane. All I need is the key."

"No way." Keith was starting to sweat, even though he could hear the soft buzz of the air conditioning unit he'd built into one wall, away from the front door and buried in a separate, small room that soundproofed the unit as well as the generators. That door was always unlocked, but there was no way to leave in that direction.

Keith fiddled with the keys in his pocket, one for the front door, one for the gun closet, and the rest for his house and car.

"I know you want to get with my mom, and that's cool. I get it. All my friends thought she was hot. With me out of the way you'll get your chance with her." Danny put his hand out. "Just give me the key."

"No way." But Keith was thinking about it. "Maybe a look around, see if anyone else is alive on the block?"

Danny smiled. "Exactly. If I find someone else alive or everyone alive I'll knock three times on the door and you let me back in."

Keith looked over at Irene, wrapped up in a thin cover on her bedroll. She looked so at peace, but he also realized he was staring at her tits through her white shirt.

"Regardless, you come back within an hour. No, make that thirty minutes. That should give you enough time to see what's going on in the immediate vicinity."

"Deal." Danny lifted a backpack from the table. "I already packed food, water and supplies."

Keith wanted to scream. He tried to keep his voice calm so they wouldn't wake Irene. "I said a half an hour, not a trip to Canada."

"Relax, old man, it's just in case. Better safe than sorry, right? I'd rather have six bottles of water on me rather than none. Besides, I know damn well that your house is packed with food and water."

Danny hefted the backpack over his shoulder. "Give me the back door key to your house."

"Hell no."

"Look, we might only have one shot at this. I'll grab some food and water, at least. We're out of toilet paper, too. I'm getting sick of wiping my ass with dishcloths and then wasting our water cleaning it."

Keith swore under his breath. As much as he hated this kid, as much as he was scared, he knew he was right. He handed Danny the set of keys. "Let me show you which key is which."

"Just show me the key to the back door of the house and I'll be fine."

"Are you sure about this?"

Danny nodded and smiled. "I've never been more sure about anything in my life, old man. I know you hate me and I sure as Hell hate you, so eventually we'd end up killing each other. Any way you look at it, fighting with me is not getting you into my mom's thong anytime soon."

Keith perked up. "She wears a thong?"

Danny laughed, making Keith feel stupid. Keith looked away but handed Danny the keys. "I'll let you out. Please be careful."

"Not a problem. Be right back."

"Thirty minutes, kid."

* * * *

Keith checked his wristwatch again and wished the kid was back so he could throttle him. It had been two hours without a sign.

Irene rolled over in her bedroll onto her side. Keith used the pen flashlight to shine a thin beam onto her ass. It didn't look like she was wearing any underwear.

She usually sponge-bathed behind the curtain but Danny was always watching him so he couldn't sneak a peek. She washed her clothes in the large basin but, again, he couldn't get close enough to see her panties or what size bra she wore.

All of this because he was weak. Weak about this woman, weak about not wanting to see what was out there, and weak about taking any action.

"Danny?"

Keith, lost in thought, jumped when Irene spoke. He stared at her. She was sitting up and her bra-less tits were bulging from the tight t-shirt, nipples erect.

"Where's my son?" she yelled and stood.

Her sweatpants hung for only a second and Keith got a glimpse of her gorgeous ass wrapped in a pink thong before she pulled them up. She turned on him with rage in her eyes. "Where is he?"

Keith shrugged and rubbed his eyes, making like he'd also just woken. "I've only been awake a few minutes. I thought he was sleeping."

Irene turned on all three lights, as if Danny would appear from the shadows and hug his mom. She picked up her jeans and a jacket before looking at Keith. "Turn around."

"Yes, ma'am." Keith turned around but counted to three before glancing over his shoulder.

Irene had her sweatpants off and was putting a leg into her jeans, her ass framed in the thong. He wanted to take her right there, thrust his manhood into her sweetness.

He turned away just as she finished getting dressed.

"I need the keys," she said.

Keith almost said that he'd given them to Danny but caught himself. He made a show of patting down his pockets. "They're gone."

"This is such bullshit, and you know it." Irene put her sneakers on. "Motherfucker let my kid walk out of this sanctuary into the end of the world."

"I didn't," Keith replied quietly, but the look she gave him and he knew she knew he was a liar. "Take some supplies."

"I don't have time for that."

Keith grabbed an empty backpack and began putting water bottles and cans of soup into it. It was full when he turned back to Irene, standing near the door.

She was smiling but it was anything but friendly. "You're letting a woman go out there alone?"

Keith just held the backpack and slowly moved it toward her.

"Why not, though, right? You let a fucking thirteen year old out by himself."

Keith looked away. He couldn't face her.

"You're a piece of shit, Keith. I hope I never see you again."

"I'll leave the door locked, but knock three times. Danny and I..."

Irene slapped him across the face and walked out, into weak sunlight.

Keith rubbed his stung face as she slammed the door, leaving him in the bunker.

Why I Write About Zombies
Armand Rosamilia

Brian Keene is the reason. End of guest blog.

Oh, you want more info?

I'd always been a huge fan of zombie movies, ever since being scared as a kid watching *Night of the Living Dead*. While everyone else was into vampires, I was the teen getting excited over zombie movies, which were hard to come by. Back in the days before the internet you had to actually go to a video store (no Blockbuster, no RedBox) down on the corner and hope that mom or pop that ran the place were fans of zombies. I remember the closest video store to me had a huge horror section, but mostly these obscure slasher flicks. I had to go a couple towns over because there was a video store that had an amazing collection of zombie movies, and I ended up renting them all.

But I'd never read any zombie books, even though I read a ton of horror. I was more into scary monster books without honing in on vampires, werewolves and zombies. Instead, demons and ghosts and serial killers were a huge part of my reading experience.

Until *The Rising*.

I remember being in the local Books A Million and searching for another paperback. The horror section had disappeared, leaving you to search through thousands of fiction books for that hidden gem deemed horror. Sure, King and Koontz had huge sections devoted to them, but everyone else was relegated to being lumped in with general fiction.

As if by fate, Brian Keene's book was facing out and the cover immediately caught my attention. I can still remember reading the back cover blurbs and being excited, because reading zombie fiction had never interested me before. The few short stories that I'd read were either about voodoo queens or cliché brain-eating zombies that had no real plot.

This was something quite different, and I read it in one day, amazed at the characters and how the zombies were not the whole story. In fact, I got so into the characters that, at times, you forgot it was even about zombies and just about survival.

I had never read anything from Keene, but went back to the store and bought every paperback he had available, including the other zombie books, *City of The Dead* and *Dead Sea*.

Within a few days I was heavily immersed in zombie fiction. I started surfing the internet for other zombie fiction, finding some great anthologies like *The Dead That Walk* and *The New Dead*.

I was also amazed at the amount of zombie authors putting out quality releases, and had to read them all.

Then I started writing my own zombie fiction, something I had never done before despite twenty years of writing stories. I thought there was nothing new, nothing fresh about it. I was wrong, and as I started thinking about my own ideas.

As a writer you never want to toss a few cliché ideas and worn plotlines together and get a story. But once I had an idea I thought was unique, I went with it. Suddenly there were more characters, more ideas than I had time to write. What started out as a simple flash fiction piece, "Higher Ground" (released in *Daily Bites of Flesh 2011* by Pill Hill Press) , became a world of extreme zombie fiction from me. Another half dozen flash fiction zombie pieces took shape, followed by my *Highway To Hell* novella. Since then I've written and published a slew of zombie short stories, followed up *Highway To Hell* with *Dying Days*, and will have a zombie short story collection out in the next few weeks (*Zombie Tea Party*).

And I owe it all to Brian Keene and that paperback book staring at me.

Armand Rosamilia

* This guest blog first appeared on *Morgen Bailey's Writing* blog at http://morgenbailey.wordpress.com/2011/10/11/ during my "Skulls World Blog Tour 2011"

Dying Days
Extreme Zombie Novella
Preview

One

Lazy Eye held the pistol to Darlene's head and licked his lips. "I said to take your fucking clothes off."

Darlene held her hands up and away from her body. "Is that a two-twenty six?"

Lazy Eye looked confused. He shook the pistol and motioned at her with his free hand. "I won't ask again."

"I think you're right about that." Darlene slipped her head down and to the left, bringing her extended fingers up and into his throat. Before he'd even stumbled she had gripped his arm, dislodged the pistol and heard his shoulder pop out of its socket.

Lazy Eye went to scream but she covered his mouth, drove her knee into his stomach, and picked up the pistol in seconds.

"Shut the fuck up or I will shoot you, motherfucker." She had no intention of actually shooting him, since they were surrounded by undead. None of them were close enough to be an immediate threat, but they were there. The gunshot would get them moving toward her for miles out here.

Under her the man struggled vainly. Darlene pointed the pistol at his head and he finally took the hint and stopped struggling. "This is a Sig Sauer 226 model, and a nice one at that. You don't strike me as being a Navy SEAL or a Texas Ranger, so I'm guessing you found it. Too bad. It's an excellent piece. Mind if I keep it?"

Lazy Eye didn't say anything. His good eye focused on her face before looking down at her dangling boobs at eye level. He licked his lips again.

"Idiot." She sat up, pulled a hunting knife from her boot and shook her head. "Here you go; the last thing you'll ever see." With that she pulled her dirty T-shirt top up and revealed her tits to the man, who openly drooled on the ground.

"Nice, I know." Darlene leaned close to him and just as his fingertip brushed against her hard left nipple she plunged the blade into his stomach and twisted. He gurgled as she drove the blade deeper into him and Darlene closed her eyes and tried to think of happy thoughts. She couldn't and began to cry softly. As much as a scumbag as this guy was, he was still living and didn't deserve to die. "Better you than me," she mumbled. She cursed herself for not hearing him sneak up on her to begin with. So busy scanning the distance for the dead she'd not heard the living until he was on her.

At this point in the game the only people still living were usually those stealthy enough, fast enough or lucky enough to keep from being ripped apart. Lazy Eye had obviously been lucky until today.

She cleaned the blade on his clothes and checked him for supplies, food, anything. He had nothing in his pockets. His boots were too big for him and he wore three pairs of socks despite being out in the Florida heat of summer. "Where did you come from?" she whispered to his lifeless body before doing the horrific task of sawing through his neck with her knife to keep him from reanimating and trying to rape her again.

He looked decently well-fed and he'd bathed in the last few days. His underwear was clean and his shirt still had a slight laundry detergent smell to it, something Darlene hadn't smelled in too long. He had a camp somewhere close, possibly a home where he had a makeshift washer.

She was in the dunes near the beach, with several undead lurking on the road behind her. Any noise would alert them. Darlene scanned the beach itself and watched as two zombies shambled from the surf and moved in different directions. They were everywhere.

Three days ago Darlene had cold-camped on a Georgia beach in a lifeguard chair. She'd woken to five zombies chasing after a child, no more than seven, down the sand. Before she could jump down and help three undead fell from the dunes behind her and gave chase as well. It was all she could do to sit in silence without making a sound as more and more came into view and went north in pursuit of fresh prey.

Now, she decided to journey the way Lazy Eye had appeared and see if she could find his camp. The going was slow, especially since she was trying to be as quiet as possible. A dead man, clothes shredded and covering only his shoulders, stumbled a few feet to her left and she froze. His penis was engorged with blood, rivulets dripping from its bloated head. He was one of the dangerous ones: the undead that still had a functioning sexual organ and would love nothing more than to use it on her, stretch her and rip into her and kill her. She shuddered at the thought.

Five tense minutes later he suddenly stopped and turned away from her and crashed through the sand toward the road. Darlene continued to move as the sun beat down upon her, sun-burnt and hurting. Six or seven months ago she was freezing, stuck in a blizzard during winter near Baltimore. She'd nearly died from sickness and watched as the living around her had succumbed to frostbite or the undead that hadn't frozen. She imagined that by now they'd thawed out and were hunting for the living.

A service road came into view, devoid of immediate danger. She joined the sandy strip up into the dunes. From this vantage point she could see for miles: A1A ran from north to south, riddled with moving bodies; a small town was to the west, smoldering and destroyed; and to the north over a collapsed bridge stood a gas station, which looked intact from this distance. She decided to make for it. Maybe there was some food left over, a stray can of soda. Crumbs would suffice at this point. Darlene hadn't eaten since yesterday morning and that meal was a rotting orange and some rain water. For weeks she'd stayed away from mirrored surfaces when possible, knowing that her once full figure was now a mess. "Even at the end of the fucking world you're still worried about how your ass looks in a tight pair of jeans," she whispered and grinned.

In order to get to the gas station she needed to traverse the broken bridge or wade through fast-moving sea water from the ocean. She didn't know if she had enough strength to make it. That had never stopped her before.

Praying to a God she no longer believed in, she moved slowly in that direction, skirting the undead and glad that they were so spread out.

She wondered why there were so many zombies concentrated in this strip of land. Once she'd gotten safely across the river and onto A1A she thought she'd be safer. With the Atlantic Ocean to the east and the river to her west, land consisted of a block or two of houses in length at any given point, but where she stood there wasn't much of anything but sand dunes. Usually the dead convened around destroyed towns, burnt-out buildings or car pileups.

There were no undead pulling themselves from the river as she stood on its banks. The bridge was unmanageable to cross, with a large chunk of it missing and presumably sitting at the bottom of the river. Darlene wondered how zombies could destroy a bridge like that, but decided that her fellow humans had most likely done the deed.

Most of the property damage she'd encountered since this had begun was man-made, with looting, raping and fires done without the zombies' help. Man had turned on man. Instead of helping one another they'd decided to kill for that last scrap of food. Safety in numbers? Not if it meant having to share a can of soup. It was easier to bash your former friend and neighbor in the head with the can rather then sharing it.

With the sun overhead and the smell of the water before her, Darlene could almost imagine that everything was normal again. Somewhere a bird actually chirped and she could almost sense the fish in the water and the ants and spiders in the grass. She was on vacation with her father, enjoying the Florida beaches and the warmth before heading back to the harsh Maine winter. They would stop later and eat at an amazing local restaurant that sold fresh seafood platters, local beer, and had tiki torches and real palm trees adjacent to the open-air dining room.

She took in a deep breath to get the rich taste of suntan oil, mixed drinks and fried fish into her nostrils. When she choked on the stench of the undead moving silently toward her she sighed. The machete strapped to her back was quietly unsheathed and she said good-bye to her father and her vacation dreams once again.

Two

He was alone and his skin was sloughing off from so much time in the seawater. His clothes were missing as well as his left arm and his hair. Darlene stepped back and took a swing with the machete, slicing through its neck like butter. She didn't even wait for him to fall before turning and stepping into the cold water of the river.

How many had she dispatched since it began? How many zombies had she destroyed? How many of the living did she have to kill as well? Barry came to mind, but he was only one of a score of men and women she'd had to fight and put down to keep from being killed herself. The first to die by her hands had been her father…

"Enough of this shit," she whispered and began moving into the water, holding her machete and two guns overhead. Luckily this was a small tributary of the actual river so she got chest-deep into it before it leveled out and she could start rising again. Her head bobbed left to right, left to right, prepared for a zombie to grip her ankle or shoot from the water. Instead, she stood on the far bank and looked around at more dunes and the sand-covered road that led to the gas station. This side of the bridge no zombies were shuffling about. She wanted to be as quiet as she could so that they wouldn't be.

As she approached the gas station she held out the Desert Eagle in her right hand and the machete swinging in her left. She was as wary about zombies as the living at this point. Friends were few and far between. Darlene figured that if there was anything of value in the gas station she'd be fighting for it. Just another day in paradise.

A chain-link fence surrounded the property, barbwire strung across the top. There was no discernable gate as far as she could see. She hated being so exposed but no trees, bushes or even dunes were between the water and the fence.

Darlene hesitated before moving to her left and away from the road leading to the gas station. Behind the property the back road wound up over another, smaller bridge, leading to a two-story house. It, too, was boxed in with the fence. The road leading between the two buildings was fenced in as well. Whoever was up in the house was probably watching her. Even now they would be getting into position with a rifle if they had one, her head in the cross-hairs. She closed her eyes and counted to five.

"I guess not," she whispered when her head didn't explode. It was almost… disappointing that she was still alive. She buried the thought in her head, swimming from the heat, lack of food and water, and the constant fear with each step she took.

To keep her mind off of it she checked and rechecked her weapons and she walked directly to the fence and stared at the gas station. If the owners were going to kill her they didn't have long-range weapons. She guessed that they'd make their way down the fenced-in road soon enough. Best see what the lay of the land was like until the confrontation.

The pumps were still intact, although sand and debris had been flung up and around them. The road itself was nearly obliterated with the natural elements as well. When Darlene noticed that the windows were unbroken and the main door complete she smiled.

Hopping the fence was no easy task in her physical state but she managed it. Her jeans had become snagged on the barbed wire and one leg was shredded. Darlene had to stop at the top and keep her head from swimming and dumping her face-first to the ground. She'd lost way too much way too fast and her muscle mass was being depleted at an alarming rate, but the alternative was much worse. She breathed in the salt air as she approached the gas station with her Desert Eagle drawn.

She hoped that the owners weren't inside.

The windows and doors had been covered from inside with cardboard. *So far, so good.*

The front door was locked as she suspected. She walked slowly around the building, trying to catch a glimpse of anything inside but there wasn't even a crack.

The bay doors to the garage area were chained and padlocked from outside, the large windows covered as well. When Darlene got to the back she glanced at the house but didn't notice any movement. For the moment there was no pursuit and no gunshots.

The back door leading into the garage was unlocked and she hesitated before turning the knob all the way and opening it. Caution made her stare intently at the door frame for tell-tale wiring or booby-traps. She didn't see anything out of the ordinary.

Six nights ago she'd come upon a camp of the living, nestled between a smoldering bowling alley and a dilapidated fast food restaurant. They had somehow dragged a damaged car into the gaps at either end and positioned guards with rifles to watch. She was pondering whether or not to reveal herself and perhaps join them when she tripped over a wire. Luckily it wasn't attached to explosives but simply to rusted cans. When it clanged the alarm three shots had rung out in quick succession in the general area that she was moments before.

The undead in the area began moving toward them. Darlene had beat a hasty retreat, dodging the undead until she could escape into a used car lot and hide in the flatbed of a Toyota Tacoma until she fell asleep. The next morning there was nothing left of the group except for blood and a few scraps of food.

"Fuck it," she whispered and turned the knob. It didn't explode, no shrapnel flew from a hidden gun, and no green glop fell from the top of the door. Silence greeted her as she stepped inside and shut the door behind her.

It was dark and she waited for her eyes to adjust to the gloom. She held her machete out just in case something dead was moving on her in the blackness.

The garage area was empty save for some grease stains on the cement floor. She hoped that a red tool setup was present so she could find a few weapons: big wrenches, hammers or even a saw. Her machete was getting dull from so much use. She'd need to sharpen it or find another weapon sooner than later.

Even though she could now see that the room was empty, she took her time and stalked around. Maybe something was hidden in a dark corner.

The only thing she found was the door leading into the rest of the gas station. It was also covered with cardboard, which she found odd. Covering the windows leading to the outside made sense.

This door was also unlocked. Again, she checked it for wires before turning the handle completely. Darlene noticed her hand was shaking. Her nerves were shot and she wondered for the hundredth times today whether all of this was worth it or not. She was physically and mentally exhausted, each day another trial and tribulation.

Darlene composed herself and shrugged her aching shoulders. "Get over it, bitch. Time to kill something."

The knob turned easily enough and she swung the door open, leading with the Desert Eagle. The first thing she noticed was the hum of the coffee makers, then the lights glowing from the soda coolers, and then the two men sitting at a table playing cards.

"Deal me in, boys," she said and realized how stupid and cliché it was. Darlene didn't care. The coffee smelled like heaven and she hoped they had cream and sugar.

Three

"Holy shit," was all one of the men could say before Darlene was upon them, holding the gun to his head.

They were both middle-aged but clean. They smelled of deodorant instead of shit. They wore coveralls and baseball caps, clean sneakers and they were clean-shaven. Darlene hadn't shaved in God-knows how long. *I could scare them with my damn bush,* she thought.

They stood in this pose for at least two minutes, Darlene with the gun to one's head and eyeing both. She had no idea what she was going to do at this point. She was too tired to take them both on and knew as soon as she pulled the trigger on the first one the second was close enough to grab her.

"Can I help you?" the second one managed, hands in the air.

"You can start by getting me a cup of that coffee."

He smiled slightly. "When was the last time you ate?"

"None of your fucking business. Move before your lover here gets his brains splattered on the floor."

"Yes, ma'am. Just relax, we can work this out." The man took three strides to the coffee pots. Darlene pressed the gun to the other's head and tried not to let him see her hand shaking.

"Never tell a woman to relax."

"Sorry," he said as he turned. He had a small-caliber pistol in his hand.

Darlene pulled the trigger on instinct and it saved her life. The explosion of his partner's head wasn't expected and his shot went wide. Darlene shot him in the stomach and he fell to the floor.

When she heard him moaning she swung around the table and leveled the gun at his head. "Move and you die."

"Too late, I think. You bitch." He tried vainly to cover the blood pouring from his midsection. His eyes were already glossing over.

She went to him, standing over him with the gun. "I can end this now or leave you here to bleed to death."

"Doesn't much matter," he choked out the words.

"Oh, but it does." Darlene leaned closer. "All I wanted was some fucking coffee."

He actually laughed at that, and began coughing and screaming in pain.

"Shut up."

He complied.

"It's your choice."

"Kill me," he managed.

"Who's at the house?"

"No one."

"Liar."

"I swear. Joe and I were the last two left. The others turned about a week ago."

"Then why were you sitting here playing cards?"

He coughed blood. She repeated the question.

"Why the fuck not? We had enough food and drink here, and the house was overrun with dead fuckers. We trapped them inside and came out here. What else could we do?"

"It doesn't look like there's a ton of food left in here."

He tried to roll onto his side but she threatened him with a kick and he stopped moving. "The bulk of the food is stacked in the house. There's enough food and water there to last a lifetime. Fucking Gary fucked up. Why did he have to go out and explore? Fuck."

"How many in the house?"

"Eight."

"What about that fucker I met before?"

"Who?"

"The asshole with the lazy eye."

He shook his head. "No idea who you're talking about. We've been cut off from everything since this shit started. We were smart enough to raid two Publix in the area for supplies."

"How is the power on?"

"Shit, the whole grid never shut off. You got power from here to St. Augustine. Fuck," he said and squirmed on the floor. "Shoot me."

Darlene pulled the trigger without preamble and shot him in the head. She hoped the fences around the building would keep the undead out. She was sure they had heard the commotion and gunfire.

At this moment she didn't care. All she wanted was a sip of the coffee. She poured a cup, added powdered creamer and chipped off a chunk of hardened sugar from a bowl, and held the cup to her nose. She remembered this smell, although she knew the coffee was stale, it had been burnt, and watered down. As soon as her tongue touched the hot brew it sent a ripple through her body. She remembered having a favorite coffee mug, a taupe one with an old, grumpy woman on the side. Below her it said '…not before my first sip…' Darlene started to weep softly as she took a seat and held the cup with both hands.

Four

The undead had heard the gunshots. They came in twos and threes, walking across the channel and standing at the fence, dripping water and body parts. Darlene counted at least twenty at one point, all directly in front of the gas station and bumping against the fence as they tried to move forward. She kept quiet and watched them through a small hole in the cardboard covering the door. After an hour most of them moved off in random directions.

Darlene chewed on her fifth and final beef jerky strip. The two men had minimal supplies. They could have survived about a week on the snacks. Four cans of soup and three vacuum-sealed packs of noodles. Darlene admired what they'd done: the coolers had been cleaned out, and the spoiled milk and flat carbonated beverages replaced by various sizes of containers of water, crammed onto the sliding shelves and stacked inside the coolers themselves. She estimated about three hundred bottles of water, enough to get her through the next six months or so. Not to mention that the faucets in the bathroom still spat water and she could easily refill as she drank.

The candy was all spoiled or stale, and she had enough cigarettes and tobacco products to get lung cancer. Despite what she'd heard, the Twinkies were actually hard. With the air conditioning still working nothing smelled, but there were only a few items that were still edible. The beer had been either finished off or raided a long time ago.

Darlene found some pink women's razors and shaving cream and ventured into the bathroom to shave and wash up. There was plenty of soap and deodorant stacked neatly under the sink, as well as washcloths and ibuprofen bottles. Before attacking the jungle that was her legs and privates she popped three pills and swallowed them with tap water. They scratched down her dry throat.

Her clothes were peeled off and dispatched to the far corner. She wouldn't have been surprised if they had suddenly stood and made a run for it. Right now she'd give anything for a bra that fit and undies that didn't have rips in them.

As she applied shaving cream she couldn't remember the last time she'd been in air conditioning. "You never get used to the smell of the dead or the smell of your own filth," she whispered. Soon the floor was stained with shaving cream, hair and dirt.

On a whim she checked the store for makeup but found none. She went back into the bathroom and finished, scrubbing her face with most of a bar of soap. For the first time in too long she stared at herself in the dirty mirror and cringed. Her cheekbones were sunken, her eyes puffy and red. Her once-lustrous hair hung in knots, her lips chapped and her chin bruised.

Darlene had never been a skinny woman – she preferred thinking of herself as curvy – but now she was downright anorexic. She guessed that she was hovering at around one hundred and five pounds, a far cry from the healthy one-fifty she normally carried. Her body was sore, black and blue covering her legs and arms, and she could spend a week counting all of the cuts across her body.

She stopped looking at herself in the mirror while she gathered her clothes and began the task of washing them under the hot water from the tap. The dirt and grime filled the sink and she noticed for the first time all of the holes and rips in her jeans and T-shirt. She'd need to find new clothing before she had to make her way naked in this dead world.

Sometimes you forget about the things you no longer have, she thought as she eyed a stack of toilet paper rolls. She was going to enjoy her time here, at least until the food ran out. Then it was back into the wild and fending for the next meal.

Later, after a dinner of cold chicken noodle soup and three bottles of water, she took both bodies outside. She didn't have the strength to bury them but figured that tomorrow she would have to. They yielded little in the way of supplies: the keys to the store, house keys she assumed were from the house up the road, a pack of gum, two pocketknives, and a dead cell phone. The small-caliber gun was empty; he'd used his last shot. She left the gun on the ground where he'd dropped it.

Darlene tossed the cell phone around in her hand and laughed. It was funny what people still clung to, even when they were of no practical use. She reached into her pocket and fingered her keychain. Her house key, her car key and the key to her dad's house were there, all useless. Yet she had them with her at all times.

She peeked outside again but there was nothing hanging around the fence. She knew they were out there. They were always out there. The glow from the coolers was enough light to see by, so she didn't have to stumble around in the dark.

Behind the counter were two pillows and three blankets, which Darlene hadn't used in months. Darlene curled up on the floor, wrapping herself in one of the blankets and stuffing both pillows under her head. It wasn't the greatest of comforts but it beat sleeping in trees, under porches and in cold abandoned buildings. Her body, newly cleaned after weeks of dipping into dirty rain water or rivers and oceans, felt relaxed. Her mind was racing and she hoped that she could sleep. *How ironic would that be, if I finally get a decent spot to sleep on, and I can't?*

She woke with a start and fought back an imaginary attacker. It was just one of the blankets that had wrapped around her legs. Her Desert Eagle, never far from her grasp, was put down on the ground next to her. While the floor had been better than being outside, her back hurt and she had a pounding headache.

By playing with the coffee machines she figured out a safe way to make two packs of the noodles and a pot of coffee for breakfast. After eating she cleaned up the store, getting everything of value together on the counter and separating the items into plastic shopping bags. In the cooler she found four cardboard boxes that could hold two dozen bottles of water each, but she had no idea how to then transport them.

Three hours later she had run out of work to do and knew that she had been stalling. She didn't want to go outside and dig two graves for the men. A part of her didn't even care about doing it, but she felt compelled. They had been alive, after all, and it would be proper to bury them and say something.

Back outside the sun was fierce, with no clouds in the Florida sky. The two bodies were right where she'd left them. She wasn't surprised, but then again not much could surprise her at this point. If they had been dancing or missing when she'd come outside it wouldn't have shocked her. In fact, it now disappointed her that she'd have to bury them. She needed a shovel, which she didn't have.

The house up the road was quiet. She wondered if they had a shed out back, and if she could keep enough distance from the house in the event that the undead inside could escape. There were no zombies outside the fence in the immediate area. Darlene decided to chance it. The sandy road leading to the house offered nothing save a few old footprints.

By the time she reached the bridge she was drenched in sweat. "I need another bath," she whispered. From here the grounds were overgrown with weeds poking through the sand. The dirt road was dusty and rutted from long-ago traffic. The front yard had, at one time, been landscaped. A section of stone wall ran the length of the driveway to the left, now showing wear in a spot and leaning back. A line of short bushes had been planted on the right, now all stunted and dead.

The house loomed before her in the midday heat like a creature ready to pounce. The windows had been boarded hastily from outside, the front door jammed with two rocking chairs and nailed shut.

Darlene was holding her breath as she put a hesitant foot on the first step. "Go around to the back," she whispered. She didn't need to be going onto the porch; she already knew what awaited her inside. She felt like the stupid chick in every horror movie that ignores the scary noises downstairs and goes into the basement, clad in her underwear, and then is amazed when an axe is sticking out of her head.

She put her full weight down on her foot. Not a sound. The wooden steps were solid. Gingerly she made it up the remaining four steps and stood at the front door with her Desert Eagle in hand. She didn't have eight bullets left – three in the Desert Eagle, three in the Sig Sauer 226 - or even know if he had been telling the truth about the number inside. Maybe it was one and he wanted to scare her away. Maybe there weren't any dead inside and the house was filled with food and drink, piles of clothing and form-fitting bras and panties with the tags still attached.

The next step forward and the boards creaked.

Darlene fell back when the banging inside started, right in front of her. It sounded like a hundred undead were inside, slamming against the wall. The windows and door shook with the impact.

Scared and ashamed at how easily she'd been rattled, Darlene ran from the porch and around to the back, in search of a shed and a shovel.

Five

As she finished burying the two men night was falling. The sounds of the trapped had brought more undead to investigate. Darlene counted almost thirty of them on the other side of the fence groaning and reaching for her. She ignored them as best she could.

At first she was going to simply walk up to them and begin smacking them with the shovel, but she knew it would be futile. The fence would keep her from doing permanent damage. In a strange way she was enjoying the company after being alone for so long. Even if her company wanted to rip off her head and fuck her headless corpse.

Back inside she drank more water and made a can of sirloin burger soup. As a kid she'd hated eating soup, but her father insisted on making it a meal at least once per week. She remembered dreading it when her parents came home from food shopping and her father stacked another three cans on the topmost shelf for later in the week.

Exhausted, Darlene checked the locks on the doors, stared into the darkness outside for lights, listened for noises, and then finally turned in for the night.

The next morning she rose, cleaned up, ate more noodle soup, and was mildly disappointed to see that the undead had moved on during the night. She wished she had binoculars so that she could climb onto the roof and see for miles.

With nothing else to do today, she ignored the still, hot air of the room and decided to clean. The undead already knew she was here so she decided to prop open the front door and the side garage door to get a nice cross-breeze flowing. Darlene supposed she could raise the large garage doors but then it might attract too much attention. The zombies weren't the only thing she had to fear; out here there was probably more than one Lazy Eye and a noise that loud would give her away.

Besides, the air felt nice when she opened the doors. She found some over-priced toothbrushes on a shelf peg and decided to give this place a thorough cleaning. A bottle of cheap bleach and some spray bottles of cleaning supplies were in the small stockroom. The mop and mop bucket were both broken and looked like they hadn't been used a long time before the end of the world. It was just as well. For the first time in months Darlene had a task besides finding food, shelter, and trying not to get killed. She dropped to her hands and knees in front of the counter and began to wash the floor, one inch at a time.

The blankets and pillows smelled funky, so they were hand-washed in the sink before she took them outside and draped them over the gas pumps to dry in the ocean breeze.

A lone zombie crested the dunes over the broken bridge, moving away from her. She wondered if they ever stopped, ever grew tired or ever had a real destination in mind when noises didn't compel them to move in a certain direction. Once again she longed for days that were long gone. In movies she used to watch with her father when she was a kid the zombies would come at night, dark and dreary, gray and overcast, with rain and lightning strikes silhouetting the background.

Darlene's reality was even more disturbing: blue, clear skies, the smell of the beach, the sound of the pounding surf, and the undead. She couldn't remember the last time it had rained since she'd been this far south. She wasn't complaining after the long, cold winter in Baltimore, but still… a little rainfall would be nice, something to break up the sun and the heat.

Once again, before going back inside to continue her cleaning project, she stepped around the side of the station and looked at the house.

It was quiet, as she knew it would be. She almost wished they'd found a way out, one at a time, so she could finish them off and grab the treasure inside. She felt like Laura Croft or Indiana Jones, only they weren't too scared to kick down the door and start shooting and killing with a trusted machete. Instead, she decided to go inside and keep scrubbing with a damn toothbrush.

At first the noise was so unexpected and so far away that she ignored it and went back inside. It seemed like a distant memory. Every now and then, especially after a fitful night of nightmares, she would sometimes wake and hear a voice or a radio playing or traffic in the distance. Fully awake she would cease to hear anything but the wind or the undead.

As it got closer she stopped and stared at the ceiling. "What the Hell?" she whispered. Back outside she stared at the sky.

She heard a plane.

"Where are you?" Darlene spun in a circle, looking and looking. There was no cloud cover. It grew louder, the sound of the engine. It might be a Cessna, something small. It wasn't a commercial airliner. *Did it matter at this point, anyway?*

Darlene couldn't remember the last time a plane, helicopter or air balloon had been spotted in the sky. She shielded her eyes from the glare and wished there was a sunglass rack inside. It made her laugh to think of her standing out here with a pair of huge white tourist sunglasses on and one of those huge weaved hats on her head.

She was positively giggling by the time the plane, indeed a Cessna, shot overhead from the west, glided straight out to sea and then shot up the coast to the north.

Immediately a score of zombies appeared and began to follow the smoke trail in the sky.

Darlene ran inside, locked up, grabbed two bags of groceries, and decided to follow.

HIGHWAY TO HELL

ARMAND ROSAMILIA

Ordering Information at

http://rymfireebooks.com/store.html

Ordering Information at

http://rymfireebooks.com/store.html

Ordering Information at

http://rymfireebooks.com/store.html

Ordering Information at

http://rymfireebooks.com/store.html

Armand Rosamilia is a New Jersey boy currently living in sunny Florida. He is the person behind Rymfire eBooks and Carnifex Metal eBooks, as well as several imprints.

His zombie novellas *Dying Days* and *Highway To Hell* have not been made into major motion pictures, graphic novels, an HBO series or used as zombie apocalypse training, although he is hopeful.

To read about his stunning life or to talk about zombies, Heavy Metal or the Boston Red Sox, find him at

http://armandrosamilia.wordpress.com

Made in the USA
Lexington, KY
29 September 2012